To Tori ____

* * *

THE TREASURE
OF HART ISLAND

Best Wishes

Mike Monahan

THE TREASURE
OF HART ISLAND

A Novel

MIKE MONAHAN

ISBN: 1546331573
ISBN 13: 9781546331575
Library of Congress Control Number: 2017907022
CreateSpace Independent Publishing Platform
North Charleston, South Carolina

Also by Mike Monahan

Barracuda

Barracuda II
The Return

Barracuda III
The Final Conflict

My name was Captain Kidd, when I sail'd, when I sail'd,
And so wickedly I did, God's laws I did forbid,
When I sail'd, when I sail'd.
I roam'd from sound to sound, and many a ship I found,
And then I sank or burn'd, when I sail'd.
I murder'd William Moore, and laid him in his gore,
Not many leagues from shore, when I sail'd.
Farewell to young and old, all jolly seamen bold,
You're welcome to my gold, for I must die, I must die.
Farewell to Lunnon town, the pretty girls all round,
No pardon can be found, and I must die, I must die,
Farewell, for I must die. Then to eternity, in hideous misery,
I must lie, I must lie.

—Author unknown

PREFACE

William Kidd was born in Dundee, Scotland, in 1645. His father was a man of the sea, so it was only natural that he took to the sea himself. By the 1680s he was an accomplished sailor and respected privateer, earning the nickname "Wizard of the Seas."

With his success, he immigrated to America and settled in New York, where he met and married a wealthy widow, Sarah Bradley Cox Oort. He continued as a privateer during the war between England and France and was commissioned to captain the *Blessed William* to protect English ships in the Caribbean from attacks from the French.

His privateering success and wealth led him into the notorious world of New York politics. The king of England appointed Lord Bellomont as governor of New York. The new governor, along with a wealthy entrepreneur, Robert Livingston, persuaded the captain to serve as a privateer who would capture pirate ships and split the booty.

Lord Bellomont and Livingston would help finance the expedition with the backing of the king of England. All pirate and French ships were fair game, and King William furnished the captain with papers allowing this privateering. The sharing of the captured cargo was a bit contentious, but the captain set out to roam the area of the Red Sea on the *Adventure Galley*.

The *Adventure Galley* was a massive three-hundred-ton ship armed with thirty-four cannons and crewed by 150 men. The ship used oars for maneuverability in battles when there was little wind. This gave the ship a decisive edge.

After a year at sea without a conquest, the crew became irritable. When the *Adventure Galley* came upon a British ship, the crew insisted on taking the boat and sharing its bounty. The motto at the time was "No prey, no pay." The only pay pirates received was the share of cargo they plundered.

British ships were off limits. The courageous Captain Kidd refused to act as a pirate and declined. An especially belligerent gunner, William Moore, became mutinous, and the captain bashed a bucket into his skull. Moore died a day later.

Soon afterward the *Adventure Galley* came upon a vessel named the *Quedagh Merchant*, which was under the protection of the French government. Since Captain Kidd had passes to take French ships, he attacked and scored a huge bounty of gold, silver, and satins. He learned later that the captain of the *Quedagh Merchant* was an Englishman, Captain Wright.

Captain Wright circulated stories that the crew of the *Adventure Galley* were pirates who tortured their captives. Soon politics and avarice combined to condemn Kidd and the crew of the *Adventure Galley*.

Captain Kidd plundered the *Quedagh Merchant* not knowing that the British East India Company owned much of its cargo. Powerful people were upset over this plunder. Based on Captain Wright's claims, Captain Kidd was declared a pirate, and warships set out for his capture.

Captain Kidd sought the safety of the pirate-friendly Madagascar. Sitting near a warm hearth and smoking Long Island tobacco from a long clay pipe, the captain looked at his first mate, Timothy Jones.

"Can ye believe t'is nonsense?"

"Yarr, it's absolute nonsense," Jones said.

"England calls me a scurvy pirate 'n' a murderer?" Captain Kidd bellowed. "Hell, I have th' French passes to prove I was within me commission to plunder th' *Quedagh Merchant*. That bastard Moore was a mutineer, 'n' I had every right to defend th' ship 'n' th' task we were commissioned fer."

He was enjoying his smoke, but he was enjoying his penny-a-glass rum even more. William Kidd was a literate and intelligent man. In his midforties, the captain was in his prime and able to best any man in his crew.

Kidd was known to have a sharp Scottish wit when sober and a fierce temper when angered. Especially when that temper was fueled by porter and rum.

He was in a foul yet pensive mood this day. He looked over his closest mates and wondered if they would follow him on his next journey.

"Tim, I have made a decision to sink th' *Adventure Galley* 'n' race a swift sloop back to New Amsterdam to answer these ridiculous piracy charges 'n' explain th' Davy Jones o' William Moore. I gonna brin' all me treasure as bargainin' chips wit' me political backers."

"Be that why we sorted all th' treasure last nightfall?" Tim asked. "I mean all th' silver 'n' gold in several chests, th' cups 'n' goblets in another chest, 'n' removin' all th' precious stones from th' jewelry pieces. I don't get it. 'N' what was that Chinese carpenter doin' to ye desk?"

Captain Kidd exhaled a lungful of smoke and smiled. He'd had the Chinese carpenter build a hidden jewelry lockbox into his huge desk, which was made in Morocco. He would hide a fortune in precious gems in this desk and have it delivered to his wife in New York.

How he missed his wife, Sarah, and his opulent home on Pearl Street with the posh riverside address. It was a three-story mansion that was built by the early Dutch. The furnishings were elegant and came from the four corners of the world. He was one of the wealthiest men in New York.

He planned to bury his privateering wealth in various locations while en route to New York to meet with his friend and backer, Lord Bellomont. The plan was to meet up with Sarah at Block Island off the point of the northern tip of Long Island. There he would off-load his desk and personal items to Sarah and her ship. She would sail back to Pearl Street while he met with Lord Bellomont, who he was told was in Boston.

Kidd knew the authorities would appropriate from Sarah any visible treasure, so he hid the fortune in jewels in a compartment of the desk, locked with a four-digit combination that only the two of them knew.

He intended to zigzag across the Long Island Sound, burying and pretending to bury treasure along the way. He would navigate to each small island at night and keep the ship far enough offshore that his crew was unaware of their location, thus ensuring secrecy.

His trusted first mate, Tim, along with two sailors would row him to shore under cover of darkness. Once on land, on Kidd's orders, the two sailors would have burlap sacks placed over their heads as they were led to a place.

Sometimes the treasure chests were filled with bounty, while other times they were filled with rocks or trash. Even Tim didn't know which was which. The two crew members would dig a ditch, place the chest at the bottom, and refill the hole.

Captain Kidd felt a sigh of relief. If Lord Bellomont betrayed him, he had the treasures to barter for his freedom. Sarah would have the real wealth secreted in the desk.

"Tim, gather th' men, load all th' treasure chests onto th' *Quedagh Merchant*, 'n' burn that leaky, worm-ridden *Adventure Galley* to th' waterline. Now that we have sold everythin' off th' *Quedagh Merchant*, let's sail her to Hispaniola."

Captain Kidd sailed to Hispaniola and attempted to sell the *Quedagh Merchant*, but to no avail. Too many mariners and investors knew that the ship was being hunted and British men-of-war were out looking for her and Captain Kidd.

Instead, Kidd used some booty to purchase the speedy sloop *Antonio*. He had the *Quedagh Merchant* scuttled after transferring his cargo to the *Antonio*. Now it was time to implement his plan to hide the treasure and negotiate for his freedom from the New York politicians and the governor. After all, they were friends and business partners.

Kidd hid his treasure chests in several locations and met his wife at Block Island. Their reunion was warm and loving but short. He transferred his personal items, including the desk, aboard her ship. They bade each other a fond farewell, and Captain Kidd sailed to Gardiners Island, a small piece of land between Long Island's north-shore and south-shore peninsulas.

The Gardiner family was quite hospitable and civil to Captain Kidd and First Mate Timothy Jones. Kidd buried treasures in a ravine between Bostwick's

Point and the Manor House. The wealth consisted of a treasure-filled chest, a box of gold, and two boxes of silver.

"T'is box 'o gold be fer Lord Bellomont. I thank ye fer ye hospitality," Captain Kidd told the island proprietor. He gave Mrs. Gardiner a length of golden cloth and a sack of sugar for their troubles.

Captain Kidd then sailed to Boston to meet with Lord Bellomont. The two met in the Boston courthouse and sat at a highly polished table.

"Lord, I have done nothin' wrong, 'n' these scandalous charges be untrue," Kidd pleaded.

"I know, my friend, but these are troubling times," Lord Bellomont said. "Piracy is all but eliminated, and the charges against you are difficult to defend against the will of the people. These charges are grave and have consequences."

Captain Kidd was immediately arrested by the court guards, who were standing at the ready. He was betrayed, and the tone of Lord Bellomont's voice told him that negotiations would be pointless.

Kidd held his head high as he was clapped into irons and placed in solitary confinement in Stone Prison. His crew was also arrested and met the same fate. They all spent more than a year in the Boston prison.

On a damp, dreary day, Captain Kidd was transported to the Boston Harbor docks and locked in a cramped space in a ship's cargo hold. The prisoner was wet, hungry, and exhausted. He had lost a lot of body weight in the previous year and knew that this long trip to England to stand trial would be horrific.

The sea was angry as the ship crashed through the waves. Kidd was tightly bound with wrist and leg irons. Caged in the schooner's cargo hold, the prisoner thirsted as undrinkable seawater swilled high against his legs and the brine stung his bloody ankles.

Pigs, hens, bales of tobacco, and other offensive-smelling cargo were crowded into this cavity of the ship. The captive had to endure hunger, thirst, and endless rolling sea swells, along with constant persecution from the crew.

"How could t'is happen to me? I be Cap'n Kidd!"

Chapter 1

The bright summer sun was creeping over the horizon like a child playing hide-and-seek. The golden rays burst into the room and woke the slumbering cat first. Before long, the hungry cat rubbed its tail in its master's face.

Mick O'Shaughnessy slowly stretched and shook out the sleep-induced cobwebs. He playfully growled at his attentive feline as he climbed out of bed. Within minutes, the cat was fed, and the coffee was on.

Soon he had coffee in hand at his computer desk. The cat, content from its meal, jumped onto the desk and was unceremoniously brushed down.

"C'mon, Mr. McGillicudy, I need to check my calendar."

There were no pressing matters on his daily log, so he decided to take a ride down to his kayak club and go for a nice paddle. Known as Micko to his friends, he often paddled for exercise on his days off from work as a detective in the NYPD.

Micko worked in a busy Bronx precinct, and a day of sea kayaking cleared his head and relaxed his tense body. Micko was not a kid anymore, but he was still a sturdy warrior to anybody who opposed him. Flecks of gray hair adorned his temples, and the strong lines in his face showed a road map of things he had seen and done.

The shower and shave were quickly done, and the early bird was soon in his vintage Pontiac Firebird riding to the New York Kayak Club on City Island, a quaint nautical village in the Bronx.

City Island is only a mile and a half long and a half-mile wide but is host to numerous seafood restaurants and nautical activities, such as speedboating, sailing, fishing, scuba diving, and kayaking. This rural community is a hidden gem of the Bronx and borders the affluent Westchester County.

Micko parked his car and unlocked the large metal gates that protected the kayak club from intruders. He quickly changed into a bathing suit and ragtag shirt and opened a shed with boat racks.

Five garage doors protected the kayaks from the elements. Micko owned two kayaks and housed them in South Shed 1.

Micko placed a pair of boat stands on the concrete deck and set his kayak between them. This was his favorite kayak. It was only twelve feet long, but it was slender and fast. The gray racing boat provided a great workout while sprinting across the waves. He adjusted the rudder and foot brace, tied down his water bottle with bungee cords, and was ready to paddle.

A large osprey flew overhead crying out for its mate. Micko was used to this ritual because the large seabirds build huge nests on the surrounding islands. The nests usually are filled with young while the parents hunt for food and keep in contact with a hail of shrilling cries.

Micko took a moment to look at the serene setting before him. The rising sun cast a golden glow across the horizon that reflected off the calm waters of the Long Island Sound. The New York Kayak Club sat on the far eastern side of City Island with an unobstructed view to the east. Several small islands dotted the water. David's Island to the north and Hart Island directly across from the club were the largest. The water was flaccid, and the many sailboats moored in the open water created a scene fit for a painting.

Micko gently picked up his kayak and carried it to the water's edge. He gracefully stepped into the craft, seated himself properly, and paddled off from the concrete dock.

He normally paddled to the southern end of City Island, then circumvented the island at a rapid pace for a nice workout. Gazing at the many harbors, marinas, and yacht clubs made for a pleasant ride.

Today, Micko decided to change routes because the early sun this time of year could be too blinding from the southeast. He would paddle around Hart Island instead.

He paddled due east a quarter of a mile and hugged the coastline. The island's trees and ancient buildings sheltered his eyes from the glaring sun. Sunglasses were rendered almost useless at this hour.

Micko paddled to the north end of the island, away from the sun, and picked up the pace for a good workout. Twenty minutes into the paddling, Micko heard the loud air horn from the ferryboat.

Each morning at eight, the ferry blew its horn to alert boaters that it was leaving the City Island dock on Fordham Street and crossing the narrow channel to Hart Island. This tender delivered prisoners from Rikers Island Prison to work on Hart Island. Most of the prisoners were short-term inmates serving time at Rikers. Hart Island is a potter's field where the indigent are buried, and these inmates dug the mass graves.

Micko checked his watch and thought, *eight o'clock. The ferry is right on time.*

Chapter 2

Flat Nose Freddie nonchalantly climbed the stairs to the top floor of the building at 2150 East Tremont Avenue. In the hallway, he looked at his watch. It was 3:00 a.m. Freddie took the last sip of his Poland Spring water and walked to apartment number 7C. *Knock, knock...knock, knock...knock.* Freddie gave the secret signal and raised the empty water bottle to the peephole. Once he heard the brass cover being released from the peephole, he raised his .38 revolver to the mouth of the water bottle.

In a moment, Frank Randazzo was dead. While a cloud of cordite hung in the air, Freddie cruised down the stairs and into the still darkness of the Bronx projects.

Freddie's father was a retired NYPD officer. When he passed away, Freddie neglected to turn in his father's service revolver with a five-inch barrel. It was as deadly today as it was decades ago. Freddie kept the weapon secured under his shirt in his father's favorite brown leather holster.

With the demise of Frank Randazzo, Freddie now controlled the drug trade in the entire Parkchester projects. Flat Nose Freddie was so named due to his unusual facial feature courtesy of a badly smashed nose. It was an epic brawl between him and Tom Monahan that ended when Monahan crashed the business end of a baseball bat into Freddie's snout. Still, Freddie was an imposing figure, standing over six feet, with wide shoulders and long, unkempt blond hair dangling past his shoulders.

Freddie earned the right to the drug trade in the other quadrants of the projects by tipping off the police on his rivals. When the top dealers sold drugs out of the housing projects, it was a complicated affair.

The dealers owned several apartments. One was for sales, one was for storage of narcotics and cash, and one was used for living quarters and cutting drugs. Each unit had a hole in the floor of a closet and an escape apartment below. If the apartment was raided, the dealers would race to the closet, jump down the hole to the apartment below, and make their escape.

Freddie knew of his rivals' intricate enterprises and covertly passed the information to the police. Randazzo was the last hurdle. Freddie now controlled the entire drug trade in this sprawling housing complex.

Learning from his competitors' mistakes, Freddie never kept large amounts of drugs or cash in any single location. He controlled ten apartments scattered about the projects and moved cash and narcotics often. If and when his operation got busted, the penalties would be minimal because of the small amount of illegal drugs at any location.

Freddie had a secret location way off site from Parkchester where he hid the bulk of his illegal contraband. He was sure nobody except his loyal soldiers would ever find out.

Flat Nose walked the six blocks to his car, parked far enough away from the scene of the murder. He made the ten-minute drive to the marina where he kept his thirty-four-foot cabin cruiser, *Who Nose*. Freddie knew things would be hot for a while, so he decided to live on his boat until things cooled down. Naturally, his minions would be selling the poison to those who craved it, so Freddie could sit tight and enjoy his budding business enterprise.

* * *

Eddie Dolan blasted the air horn from high upon his perch on the ferryboat *Ichabod's Crane*. The huge twin diesel engines were already churning the water into a furious foam as he put the ship into gear. Dolan had been the pilot for these Department of Corrections tenders for twenty years. He looked down at the two white vans that held the prisoners in check until they arrived at the Hart Island dock. The large yellow box truck held the remains of deceased homeless in plain pine boxes. *The inmates will be busy today,* he mused.

Andy Hastings was pacing the deck as the ferry slowly pulled away from City Island. He had another fight with his wife that morning, and as usual it was over money. Andy had twenty-five years of service as a prison guard and was ready to retire, but his wife's lifestyle kept him cash-strapped.

The love was long gone, as were the kids. Now was supposed to be his time to retire and enjoy the golden years. Andy was short, balding, and overweight, but he still had a sparkle in his eyes. His wife found more enjoyment in the casino at Yonkers Raceway than in her household obligations. This led to a dirty house, fewer home-cooked meals, and poverty-induced fights.

Manny Santiago walked up to Andy and said with a laugh, "Penny for your thoughts."

"It's Peggy again," he said.

"How can anyone always lose at those machines? Even a mental case has to win sometime," Manny said.

"She is a mental case and still can't win. I don't think I'll be able to retire this year."

Manny put his arm around Andy and said, "Hey, man, you know I can't afford my old lady either. She wears fancy clothes and jewelry, so I have to work a second job tending bar."

Andy laughed. He knew Manny had his hands full with Maria. She was a gorgeous, high-spirited lady with champagne tastes living on a beer budget. Manny worshipped the ground she walked on and gave her anything she desired. She was the prettiest gal in the hood, and Manny had mediocre looks. Andy knew that spoiling the extravagant Maria was the only way Manny could keep her.

The *Ichabod's Crane* slowly trolled across the narrow strait. It was a workhorse of a boat that had seen better days. The ferry was long enough to transport several cars and construction equipment and had a built-on crane for heavy lifting.

The current can be tricky when the tide changes, but Eddie Dolan was a master pilot and eased the ferry into the Hart Island dock.

The yellow box truck exited first, followed by the two white prison vans. Andy drove one van and Manny the other. They pulled up to an ancient red-brick building that housed the construction tools and machines necessary to dig the trenches for mass burials. There were also gardening apparatuses that the prisoners used to landscape when they had light burial days.

Today they would be busy digging graves, so the prisoners ignored the gardening shed and went straight for the burrowing tools. Each van contained five prisoners, the driver, one armed guard, a wicker basket containing lunch supplies, and a water cooler.

The Halpin brothers, John and Neil, were the Department of Corrections armed guards. They loved working away from the mindless cellblocks at Rikers Island Prison. On the burial detail, they were outdoors, worked steady day shifts with weekends off, and had at least two hours of overtime per day. Their wives and children were happy with this arrangement.

The prisoners on this cozy detail were short-term detainees who had been well screened. Besides the pay of fifty cents an hour, many perks came with long days outside the prison walls.

John Halpin took the keys to the SUV and threw them to Neil in the modified golf cart.

"Our orders for today state that van number one will work the babies' cemetery and van number two will work adult section 440C," John said.

The Halpin brothers took turns with the vehicles that were kept on the island. The SUV was used to patrol the perimeter. Although numerous warning signs were posted in high visible areas, boaters, kayakers, and Jet Ski riders would beach their craft. The guard in the SUV warned them away while the brother in the golf cart kept a watchful eye on the prisoners.

The yellow truck drove to section 440C grave site with the two white vans following. All ten prisoners helped unload the fifteen plain pine adult boxes and spread them on the ground. The truck drove to the other side of the island to the sacred children's section marked with a large white stone cross. There were only four small baby boxes on the truck, so Manny told Andy he would have his five men unload them.

The small infant graves were respectfully hand dug by shovel, while the adult graves were plowed with the use of a backhoe. The tiny coffins were handled gently, while the larger, heavier adult boxes were manhandled into place and stacked into deep trenches. The coffin numbers were logged in a detailed records book.

This was the first time in a week that the prisoners were allowed on the island since a heavy rainfall. The earth was still wet, and digging was easy. The four baby coffins were quickly hand buried and covered with the use of a Bobcat. Manny told his men to take a break while the empty yellow box truck drove back to the ferry for its ride back to City Island.

Manny handed the children's grave-marker ledger to Neil Halpin and said, "I'm going to see if Andy needs a hand." Neil nodded while he looked over the grave ledger.

"The soil is so wet; the grave walls keep falling in on themselves," Andy said to Manny. "This will take all day."

"Why not try digging in a different spot?" Manny said.

"The schematic points to this specific spot for today's burials. The engineers come out here once a month and plot out where to place the bodies on a daily basis."

"Well, screw that. Just move over one section and mark it in the ledger, Andy."

"All right. Rickey, move that machine over to the right, one section, and try digging there," Andy yelled to the backhoe operator.

Rickey Torres worked construction before he stabbed his boss. The wound wasn't mortal but critical enough to get Rickey one to three in Rikers Island Prison.

Torres moved his machine as ordered and began to dig into the soft soil. The hole wasn't more than four feet deep when he yelled, "Hey, Andy, the engineers screwed up. I just hit a casket here."

Torres backed up his machine and jumped down from the cab to join the others looking into the fresh pit.

"Joe, jump in and see what that is," Andy said.

Joe Jackson was an auto mechanic who found that car thefts paid better. He was in the last month of his stretch at Rikers. Jackson jumped into the wet hole and began digging around the object with his bare hands. The soft earth gave way easily, and a startled Joe Jackson exclaimed, "Holy shit!"

Just then, the muddy walls of the grave slid down and buried Joe in a heap of muck. Andy immediately threw shovels to the remaining prisoners and ordered them to quickly dig Joe out of the hole before he suffocated.

The rescue was successful, and a filthy but unharmed Joe Jackson begged for water. After he drank his fill, he became wide eyed.

"There's an old chest down there."

Chapter 3

The salty sea spray splashed off the bow and into Micko's face, making him feel alive. He loved to plow through the waves at full speed to get this effect. He noticed several boats with fishermen heading out to sea to earn their living while huge oil tankers crept toward New York Harbor at a snail's pace.

Micko observed everything around him, and there was a lot to see. Numerous species of seabirds flocked to this area, along with Canada geese, swans, and cormorants. They all ignored him as they swam or fed or just flocked together on the surface.

The aerial maneuvers were most intriguing when the birds dove from high above and went deep for their quarry. The albatross and hawks showed off their flying skills as they taught their young to hunt.

Entering the many marinas and observing the various yachts and recreational boats were pleasant parts of his workout. City Island had many marinas, and Micko enjoyed muscling his twelve-foot yacht around them, except today. Today he powered his gray kayak around Hart Island.

There had been a week of storms, and Micko noticed a few new wrecks washed up on the Hart Island shoreline. When heavy winds dislodge ill-secured boats from their moorings, the boats are pushed along until they wash up somewhere. Hart Island was often their graveyard.

Micko was glistening with sweat as he sprinted the final one hundred yards to the concrete dock of the kayak club. He was exhausted and knew he had a good workout. He remembered, *it's easier to climb into a narrow kayak than it is to climb out, especially when you are dog tired.*

Micko tried to climb out gracefully but instead executed a "wet exit" as he stumbled into the knee-high water.

"I thought you were the expert kayaker around here," a voice bellowed.

Micko thought he was alone. He blushed as he turned to see Bill Gerhard sitting in a small outboard skiff laughing hysterically.

Bill was a friendly, opulent guy who owned Gerhard's Marina adjacent to the New York Kayak Club. Bill apparently observed Micko paddling back to the club, so he motored over for some conversation.

"I may fall out of a kayak, but you could never fit into one," Micko said, laughing.

"Why would I ever want to climb into that tiny thing when I have a nice, comfortable sixteen-foot motorboat?" Bill returned with a laugh.

Micko regained his composure and carried his small craft to the kayak racks on the clubhouse deck. He returned to Bill and helped him secure his boat dockside.

The two engaged in a comical conversation while Micko washed down his kayak and returned it to its berth.

"Hey, Bill, how about giving me a ride over to Hart Island so I can scuba dive for some lobster and clams? I'll share my catch with you."

"How long will you be?" Bill asked.

"I have my dive gear in my locker—I was going to clean it today—but as long as you have your skiff, I will catch us dinner. I'll be out in five minutes."

Micko often hunted for dinner in these fish-friendly waters. Lobster and clam hunting required only a steady hand, a goody bag, and sharp reflexes. When hunting for blackfish, Micko used a Hawaiian sling spear.

Ten minutes later, Micko had his dive gear loaded into Bill's boat, and they motored across the channel toward Hart Island.

* * *

Once Andy was sure that Joe was all right, he told the rescuers to go back into the hole and secure the chest. They enthusiastically did as they were told and quickly uncovered the ancient wooden trunk.

"That looks like it will fall apart if we try to lift it, Andy," Manny said.

"Schirabba, can you get a sling around it so we can raise it with the backhoe's front-loader shovel?" Andy asked.

Mike Schirabba is a "made man" in the Morris Park Mafia clan. The feds had been after him for a long time but could nab him with only a handful of policy slips. His sentence of three months was up in one week. He would normally have objected to jumping into this mire, but the box intrigued him.

"Yeah, give me that fat mother of a sling. I'll stick it under the chest, and it should cradle it all right," Schirabba said.

The chest was closed and appeared to be locked. Schirabba worked furiously to slide the thick sling under the heavy load.

"Lift slowly and gently," he ordered.

Rickey had turned the backhoe around so that the front loader was facing the ditch. Manny attached the other end of the sling to the front shovel, and the lift began. Just as the chest was rising, it split at one of the lid hinges, and coins spilled out.

"Gently," Schirabba said.

Prisoners Jerry Mooney and Ralph Quinones scrambled to pick up the spilled coins. Andy screamed, "Leave those alone and grip the chest together with your hands, you assholes!"

Mooney and Quinones cradled the bottom of the box as Schirabba helped guide it to the pit's muddy edge. Rickey expertly lowered the chest onto a pile of muck, and they all gathered around for a look.

It was immediately apparent that this was buried treasure, based on the age and condition of the chest, coupled with the unfamiliar coins sticking out of the split hinge.

The prisoners were arguing about splitting the bounty when Andy jumped in. "Quiet! There are seven of us here. We don't want anyone else to know about this."

All eyes were on Andy when he slowly said, "We will hide the chest inside one of the old abandoned buildings. We'll cover it with a ton of mud until we can figure out what to do. Rickey, scoop the front loader under the mud beneath the chest and carry mud and chest to the old rehab building."

Rickey did as he was told and carried the mud and chest to the derelict remains of the Phoenix House for substance abusers. He returned three times with enough mud to completely hide the chest from prying eyes.

Andy called the men to his side. "Do not tell a soul about this find. Since Joe is banged up and the rest of you are filthy, I will radio the ferry to take us back to Rikers to clean up. We will then make a plan as to how to recover and sell this treasure. Do not tell anyone!"

Andy took Manny aside and whispered, "Look, Manny, you stay here with your gang at the children's cemetery. Let the guards know how my gang got messy with the cave-ins and that I'm bringing them back to Rikers. I'll meet you at Hurley's bar at the end of our tour to discuss the treasure."

* * *

Micko crashed through the surface of the water ten feet from Bill and his boat.

"I got us dinner, Billy Boy," he shouted as he waved his yellow mesh goody bag high in the air.

Bill could see at least four lobsters and a handful of clams in the bag.

"I hope you have a lobster license, Detective." Bill grinned.

A few minutes later, Micko was clambering aboard the small boat when he noticed the ferry pulling away from City Island and heading back to Hart Island.

"That's funny. The ferry makes an 8:00 a.m. drop-off, comes back to City Island, then goes back for a pickup at three p.m. This is an unscheduled trip. I wonder what's up," Micko said.

* * *

After Manny left with van one to meet his five prisoners at the baby cemetery, Andy gathered his flock and drove to the ferry dock. The ferry was already there. Andy stopped short of the pier and again told the men, "Don't tell a soul about our find."

The prisoners were agitated and arguing about who got what percentage of the booty and if Andy and Manny could be trusted. This worried Andy. The veteran Department of Corrections prison guard saw a way out of his miserable life, and these ignorant bastards could jeopardize everything. In an instant, prison guard Andy Hastings knew what he had to do.

Andy slowly drove the prisoner van across the dock and onto the rear of the ferry. One of the tender workers pulled in the retractable ramp and latched the stern safety chain. He gave a signal to Dolan, and the ferry plowed off into the channel.

* * *

Micko was slipping out of his dive gear while Bill hauled in the anchor. Bill was bragging about his seafood-cooking abilities when Micko said, "Shit, did you see that?"

Bill gave his buddy a quizzical look.

"The ferry. A van just rolled off the back and into the water!" Micko yelled.

Without another word, Bill quickly stowed the anchor, put the outboard in gear, and headed for the ferryboat. Micko realized it must have been a prison van that was probably full of trapped cons. He swiftly suited up for a rescue dive.

"Bill, open that toolbox."

"What do you need?" Bill asked.

"Any kind of pry bar or something."

Bill opened the box and said, "All I have is a heavy-duty claw hammer."

"That will do."

Dolan was made aware of the situation and circled the area of the mishap. Andy was spotted splashing wildly in the waters churned up by the powerful twin engines of the ferryboat.

Micko and Bill quickly arrived on the scene, and Micko yelled, "*Ichabod's Crane*, back off before you drown this man with your wake. We will pick him up in our boat."

Andy knew he had to make this look good, so he swallowed a lot of water as he allowed himself to be dragged into the small boat by his two rescuers. Andy coughed up a load of phlegm and acted as if he were half-drowned. When Micko and Bill were certain the man would be all right, Bill dropped anchor.

"Micko, do you have enough air?"

"I hope so. I just don't know how deep it is here."

A continuous explosion of surface bubbles indicated the location of the van, giving Micko a direction to dive. He took a moment to recheck his gauges and equipment and lowered himself over the side of Bill's boat.

Micko normally would descend slowly, taking caution in unknown areas of the Long Island Sound. This was different, and speed was of the essence. Micko hoped the prisoners were in the van, trapped with a large air pocket. If he could reach them before the air bubble was exhausted, there was a chance for a rescue.

The tide was coming in at a vicious rate, and Micko had trouble diving against it. At thirty feet underwater, he was able to see the white vehicle. It took another twenty feet to reach the van, which was sitting upright.

Micko swan to the van from the front and saw that the driver's window was down, and the door was open. This allowed water to immediately fill the van and sink it quickly. Micko made a mental note of this and noticed that the gear was in reverse.

The prisoner van was the typical rear-loading type with a metal cage separating cons from the guards in front. Micko could get into the front seat but would be unable to reach the men trapped in the rear. He swam swiftly to the rear and used the hammer claw to pry open the doors.

The cheap lock gave way easily, but the current was so swift that it pushed up against the doors, hindering Micko's ability to gain entry. Using all the strength he possessed, Micko finally won the tug-of-war and opened one of the doors. He was immediately pushed inside by the rushing water.

Time seemed to stand still as Micko was cast into a room of blinding darkness. He was tumbling as if stuck in a washing machine. Knowing his air level was seriously low, the blinded and tumbling detective felt a wave of fear wash over him.

Then he remembered the scuba diver's creed for danger:

Stop
Think
Act

Micko let himself tumble for a minute as he tried to assess his situation. He dove in haste to reach the van and never pulled out his flashlight from his buoyancy vest pocket. He retrieved the light and turned it on.

The scene before him was surreal: five men tumbling like rag dolls within the confines of their final jail cell. Like apparitions from a watery hell, the men stared blankly with slackened jaws while doing a hideous dance of death.

Micko found a hand grasp on the metal partition to steady himself. The dancers floated with the surge, limbs all akimbo, flailing wildly. Micko was mesmerized but trapped.

He spotted a shiny object on the floor of the van. He grabbed it and placed it into his buoyancy vest pocket before the surge pushed it away.

He checked his air level again and knew he was in real trouble. Micko made a decision that would be questioned by divers for years. He desperately climbed out of his bulky dive gear to become more streamlined and took one last deep breath before hurtling himself toward the rear door during one of the outgoing surges.

Micko reached the door and held on for dear life during the incoming surge. Still holding his breath, he pushed with everything he had to squeeze through the door on the next outward surge.

He kicked clear of the wreckage and made an emergency ascent, slowly rising to the surface and exhaling. By dropping his dive gear, he became more aerodynamic and able to torpedo through the rushing water to reach the exit door. As long as he rose to the surface slower than his bubbles, he would likely not be hit with the deadly and painful bends.

Micko breached the surface hundreds of feet from Bill's boat and was pushed by the current toward the ferry dock at the end of Fordham Street on City Island.

Bill was frantically searching the waters for any sign of Micko's exhaust bubbles, but with the steady stream of foam from the van, it was impossible to spot the tiny air bubbles of a diver.

"Look, there he is," said Andy, pointing toward shore.

Andy and Bill saw dockworkers pulling Micko onto the ferry berth. Bill observed that Micko was without his dive gear and realized it must have been hairy down at the crash site.

Chapter 4

Flat Nose Freddie was running scared. There had been three homicides in the projects in the past month, and police activity was high. He knew his boat and the marina were not safe. He absolutely refused to leave town and his lucrative drug empire unattended, so he improvised.

Some time ago, while entertaining girls on his boat the *Who Nose,* Freddie would occasionally anchor on the east side of Hart Island, out of sight from the curious City Island residents. Freddie decided to explore this island one night. Everyone knew it was forbidden, but the corrections people left the island at three o'clock, and it was unattended on weekends. The local police harbor units gave it special attention, but only if they were around that area.

Freddie's right-hand man, known only as Itchy, had knowledge of the island from his days in the telephone company. Itchy would keep the island's minimal phone service operable.

Itchy was a short, stocky man who developed a serious heroin addiction while employed by the phone company and was let go as a result. Itchy and Freddie were childhood friends, and the two hooked up years later in Freddie's early dealer days. The two became inseparable. Whenever he needed a fix, he became itchy and would scratch his hands and neck—thus the nickname.

While the Corrections Department used much of the island as a potter's field, many unused and unexplored facilities were scattered about. Freddie planned to make use of these facilities with Itchy's help.

During the Cold War era, the US Army built a series of missile silos on Hart Island. These were abandoned years ago, but the silos, underground passages, and hidden storage facilities were still there.

This was where Flat Nose Freddie decided to hide much of his illicit-drug activity, far from the Parkchester projects where his enemies were hunting him. Freddie and Itchy, with the help of their drug-addicted slaves, made the uninhabitable hidden rooms habitable again.

All those who helped Freddie rebuild this army facility mysteriously overdosed on heroin. Freddie would just lace a dose with extra fentanyl, and another addict died without much fanfare or publicity.

This was where Freddie decided to lie low until the overworked police moved on to other matters. Itchy would oversee the Parkchester drug empire while Freddie stored huge amounts of heroin on Hart Island to supply dealers from New York to Canada.

Deliveries were made from boat to boat from this uninhabited NYC-owned property on popular tourist waterways. It was foolproof. Freddie could afford to lose his Bronx project empire and still be the king of NY heroin.

Text messages were sent to Freddie with dates and times, and cash and drugs were exchanged in a small cove near Sands Point, ten miles offshore from Freddie's hideaway on Hart Island. The buyers cut his heroin and transported it along the coast to Canada.

It took Freddie and Itchy two years to comfortably occupy the hidden parts of Hart Island right under the noses of the guards and prisoners. Itchy used his knowledge of wiring to replace the ancient fuse boxes and rewire the vast underground connecting rooms.

Freddie had electricity running to all the essential rooms but used it sparingly lest some bean counter spot a spike in energy use from Hart Island. Energy-efficient battery-operated LED lights were placed in all compartments. Storage units were filled to capacity with survivalist products: food, batteries, lighters, candles, and propane-gas stoves.

Freddie's personal living quarters were fit for a king. The large refrigerator was always well stocked. This was the only device that sucked up electricity, but Flat Nose hoped it would not be enough to attract attention. The corrections people used pure electricity, while Freddie relied on generators most of the time.

Freddie always unplugged coffee makers, television sets, and other non-essential items while he was away. Still, his underground kingdom was more comfortable than most high-end hotels.

This is where Flat Nose Freddie decided to cool his heels until the heat was off. Itchy could watch over the daily operation in Parkchester while Freddie maintained his lucrative export business from his hideaway.

His people in the projects cut and packaged his distinctive brand of heroin. The poison he sold to the inner-city kids of the Bronx was stamped with the brand name King. The exported heroin was stamped with a red heart. Both brands were in great demand. Freddie cut the less-pure Bronx heroin with a dash of fentanyl to give a greater rush to its users. The exported Red Heart was in a purer state that was left to the buyers and dealers to cut in any way they saw fit.

Freddie worried about his loyal pal Itchy, who was a functioning heroin addict. He was always in control when he was needed and sneaked away to shoot up when not needed.

* * *

Micko was prostrate on the ferry dock, still trying to catch his breath, when a crowd began to assemble. The narrow Fordham Street that leads to the pier was quickly filling up with emergency vehicles. Ambulances, police cars, and fire trucks all jockeyed for position. Micko knew that before long, first-responder bosses would arrive, along with the news media, turning this accident into a spectacle—if it was an accident.

Bill was attempting to tie up his boat at the ferry dock when Micko yelled, "Bill, don't tie up. Take me back to the kayak club."

"What about this guy?" Bill asked, pointing to Andy.

"He's coming with us."

Micko climbed into Bill's boat, and Bill drove the short distance to the New York Kayak Club, where the three exited the boat and sat at a picnic table. Micko went into the clubhouse and returned with three beers and a pad and pencil.

"My name is Detective Mick O'Shaughnessy, and I want you to tell me everything that just happened," he said to the rescued guard.

"Shouldn't I have my union lawyer present before I say anything?" he asked.

"Listen, I just lost my expensive scuba gear and nearly my life, so speak up!" Micko commanded.

The man said his name was Andy Hastings, a twenty-five-year veteran Rikers Island guard. He told a tale of his men being covered in mud from a burial mishap and one who was possibly injured. He explained that he was taking them back to the prison for a cleanup and health checkup. Andy got a bit emotional when he said he drove the van onto the ferry and somehow must have put the gear into neutral when he thought it was in park. The van was on an incline and backed right off the rear of the ferry after snapping through the simple chain-link guardrail.

Micko watched the man closely. Andy had trouble looking him in the eye. The wet guard also looked down and to the left during critical parts of the story. Seasoned detectives know what this means: the story doesn't match the body language.

Micko took notes and called a friend in the Forty-Fifth Precinct detective squad. He was told that Jack McCarthy caught the case, and the call was transferred to his desk.

"Hey, Jack, Micko here."

"How are you, Micko? To what do I owe this pleasure?" Jack asked sarcastically.

Jack McCarthy was a veteran detective who usually snatched the newsworthy cases because of his expertise. The two detectives didn't get along well. Jack was harsh and abrasive to all who knew him. He took cases that were self-serving, and he degraded any detective who complained.

He was a twice-divorced cop with years of alimony payments left to both ex-wives and was overall a miserable man.

"I'm fine, Jack. I'm down here at City Island at the scene of the incident."

"I'm on the way there now. Micko, it falls into the jurisdiction of the Forty-Fifth Precinct."

"Jack, don't go straight there. Meet me at the New York Kayak Club. I can better fill you in here than at the circus on Fordham Street."

"See you in ten," Jack said.

*   *   *

Manny drove back to where his men were having a peaceful lunch. The Halpin brothers were nowhere to be seen, probably sneaking a drink. He was too excited to eat, and his mind was racing with wild thoughts. *I wonder how much money we can get. How do we split it? Who do we sell this stuff to without getting caught? Can I trust these guys? Will they keep their mouths shut?*

The Halpin brothers rode up in a cloud of dust from the SUV. John yelled, "Gather your things. We are going to the ferryboat dock."

Manny calmly asked, "What's up, guys?"

"There has been an accident with the ferry. The other prisoner van slipped off the rear, and all sorts of bosses are arriving," Neil said.

Manny gathered his men and drove to the pier. As everyone else watched the activity on the water, Manny slipped away from the group.

He took a stroll around the grounds in a pensive mood. Shortly, he knew the answers to his questions and opened his cell phone.

"Maria, listen very carefully to me, my love."

Manny ensured he was well out of earshot as he explained the events to Maria. He hated bringing in the gangsters from her past but felt he had no choice.

*   *   *

Micko opened the gates to let Jack into the kayak club and motioned for him to sit at the picnic table. He quickly introduced Jack to Bill and then explained the day's events.

"Is that the guard?" Jack demanded, pointing to a wet man making a cell phone call near the water's edge.

"Yes, that's him. He's calling his union delegate."

"Let's talk to him quick before he's advised to lawyer up," Jack grumbled.

As Jack interviewed Andy, Micko went to his locker. He cleaned up himself and brought out dry clothes and a towel for Andy.

Andy appreciated the gesture as Micko hung out their wet clothes to dry on the club's flagpole. Jack knew Micko was gaining the guard's trust and friendship with these acts of kindness.

Andy looked silly in a tight T-shirt and undersized bathing suit, but at least he was dry. Micko brought out another round of beers and a coffee for Jack. He stayed away from the interview because he wanted to compare notes with Jack.

Andy walked back down toward the water to make another phone call as Micko and Jack compared notes. There were numerous inconsistencies, and Jack started preparing questions for a second interview for clarification at a later time.

Micko believed that Andy was lying and drove the van off the ferryboat either carelessly or on purpose. Neither detective could figure out why he would do it on purpose. Jack wanted to close the case as an accident. Micko wanted to interview various people to learn if Andy had a beef with any or many of the deceased inmates.

Just as Micko was walking Jack out the gates, a large limo pulled up. Jack moaned, "Oh no, it's the chief of detectives."

COD Dennis Clifford stepped out of the limo with an indisputable air of authority. He looked pleasurably over the marine landscape and then growled at the detectives, "Fill me in and make it fast. I just left a lovely dinner engagement."

Micko let Jack do the talking since it was his case. Clifford listened intently and asked, "In your opinion, is this an accident or foul play?"

The two detectives glared at each other. Jack said he wanted to refer the case to the inspector general of the Department of Corrections to investigate as an unfortunate accident.

Micko, however, thought the case needed to be thoroughly investigated. There were too many inconsistencies in the guard's story, and five men were dead.

Clifford was impressed by Micko's role in this incident and took him aside.

"Micko, I'm going to let McCarthy pass this to the Rikers IG, but I also want you to investigate. There is more here than meets the eye."

Micko silently smiled when the NYPD chief of detectives called him by his first name. They had a cordial relationship ever since Micko's cases in the South Pacific met with favorable results.

Clifford continued. "You will work conjunctively with the DOC, but also independently, reporting to me alone. I will assign you as part of a joint operations task force. This will give you complete access to all DOC files, properties, and personnel."

Micko asked, "Why me, Chief? This isn't even my precinct."

"You are already personally involved, you know all the incidentals of this case, and, frankly, you have proved yourself in the past." Clifford smiled warmly at the detective.

"By the way, you're on this case as of now, so start investigating while I make the necessary phone calls."

Chapter 5

"I understand, baby." Maria hung up the phone and thought for a long moment before she dialed. No answer. Maria would not leave a message on the answering machine. This was too private.

Mundo was playing pool with his crew at their South Bronx clubhouse when the phone rang. He looked at the number and saw it was Maria.

Now what dat bitch want? he wondered.

Maria and Mundo were an item several years ago, but as Mundo rose in the ranks with the Black Outlaws, he passed her off to all his crew members.

She was an attractive whore but too needy. Now he only occasionally gave her a pop when he needed a quickie or info on imprisoned gang members from her prison-guard boyfriend. The Black Outlaws had enough whores around to keep the crew satisfied.

On the fourth call, curiosity got the better of him. "Hello, sexy, you be horny?"

"Always for you, baby, but I have a way for us all to become rich," she cooed.

Maria explained to Mundo all Manny had told her. It was also Manny's idea to have the Black Outlaws get to the loot before anyone else did. Maria described where the treasure was hidden and how to get there.

"Baby, you need a boat, and at three a.m., land it on the small beach on the east side of Hart Island. It's the only beach area there. Then walk inland until you see the cemetery. The chest is buried under a pile of mud inside the third red-brick building on the right. Manny says don't use flashlights until you are indoors."

"Hart Island? What de fuck is Hart Island?" an irritated Mundo snarled.

"Manny says it's that island across from Orchard Beach, only you go to the opposite side of the island for the booty." She giggled.

Mundo remembered the sex they had at Orchard Beach, and now he knew which island was Hart. He had to get a troop together to go to City Island, sneak into a marina, and steal a boat for the operation.

* * *

Andy's first call was to his union delegate, who listened to his tale and told him he would contact the union lawyers and get back to him. After Detective McCarthy's interview, Andy crept down toward the water's edge and called his fellow Rikers guard Lynch Turner.

William Turner was a younger guard who got the nickname after one of the prisoners in his charge hanged himself with a shirtsleeve. Lynch came from a troubled past and continued his troubles while a guard in Rikers. A strong union kept him from being fired, but he was given the worst prison assignments.

Andy knew that Lynch had contacts who would do nefarious things. That's why Lynch knew so many inmates personally. Andy knew this was the man he could trust.

"Lynch, my fellow IRA bastard, how are you?" Andy yelled into the phone, knowing his pal would be in the noisy courtyard.

"I'm fine, fine. Let me get to a quieter spot, Andy."

A few minutes later, Lynch said, "Hey, what's up, boyo?"

Andy trusted his Irish Patriot with his life. He briefly explained the situation and the need to quickly remove the treasure before he was betrayed. Lynch was all ears and asked Andy to go into greater detail.

When Turner had all the facts, he groaned. "But Andy, I'm stuck doing a double shift as punishment for gambling with the cons in C Block."

"Lynch Turner, you listen to me. You get a gang out there tonight, or else we lose everything. I don't have your deplorable contacts, or else I'd call them."

"All right. I'll get someone to cover for me for a bit and make some calls to guys I trust and are up to the job."

* * *

Now that he was officially assigned to the case, Micko had to get dressed in his street clothes and walk the six blocks to Fordham Street. He would have to speak with numerous people from the DOC and observe the recovery of the van.

The scene at Fordham Street was still chaotic, but Micko had his detective shield around his neck and easily got access to the various bosses. He left Andy with the DOC investigators after he explained to them all he knew and took names and phone numbers for his reports to come later.

Two NYPD harbor units were on the scene, and Micko had a small DOC dinghy ride him out to the ferryboat. That was where he met Detective Mike Crew, who was in charge of the van recovery.

"Mike, how the hell are you?"

"What the heck are you doing here?" Crew asked.

"I was diving for lobsters when I saw the accident. I tried to rescue the prisoners trapped in the van, but I only managed to lose my dive gear." Micko blushed for the second time that day. Divers are not supposed to lose their dive gear underwater.

"You lost your what?" Crew asked.

"Bad current, long story," Micko said.

"Yeah, that's why I'm having my recovery team wait for slack high tide to go down. The water will be much calmer, and we will have the bodies and van up in a jiffy—unless you let the bodies out and they got caught in the current."

"No, they are spinning like tops inside the van. I barely got out myself, and the current shut the door behind me when I did exit."

Now Mike Crew knew how Micko lost his gear and realized how harrowing it must have been, especially attempting a solo rescue.

The two detectives gabbed for another hour before the slack tide arrived. The NYPD divers attached a wide sling to the ferry's crane and entered the water. They were wearing Aga full face masks with a communications system installed so they could speak to one another and to the surface. Within minutes, they let Crew know they were ready for the sling. Crew motioned to Eddie Dolan, who expertly operated the crane and lowered the sling. Two divers met the sling at the surface and guided it down to the two divers at the wreck scene.

Fifteen minutes later, the van was slowly being hauled to the *Ichabod's Crane*'s rear deck. It took a full ten minutes for the water to drain out of the van, before anyone could get inside.

The force of the current and Micko's prying had warped the rear doors, so entry was difficult without the Jaws of Life cutting tool. When the doors were forced open, Micko and Crew climbed inside. The five cons looked like water-soaked dolls lying askew on the floor of the van.

Micko searched each body. With Crew's help, he carried them out to the ferry's deck and laid them out on a canvas sheet. The cons had nothing on them except their work clothes.

Crew directed Dolan to move the ferry to the Fordham Street dock, where an ambulance staff would declare the cons dead and note the time of their finding. Then the waiting medical examiner's mortuary van would transport the bodies to the Jacobi Medical Center's morgue for autopsies.

Micko retrieved his dive gear and was eager to get back to the kayak club to check it for damage. He couldn't examine it on the scene without appearing insensitive.

Detective McCarthy was doing a cursory investigation and collecting names for his reports, which would declare this incident an unfortunate accident. The DOC bosses were happy about this. They just wanted this entire incident to go away.

Micko was more thorough. This pissed off a lot of people, and they let him know—especially when he told Dolan to take the ferryboat back to Hart Island so he could interview the staff from van one.

With the water-soaked van and bodies removed, Mike Crew asked to be dropped off at one of the NYPD harbor boats at the crash scene. Dolan was powering the *Ichabod's Crane* when Micko asked, "Mike, did you notice the position of the gear shifter in the van when we brought it on deck?"

"I sure as shit did. It was in reverse."

"Make sure you note that in your report, Mike, OK?"

"Sure thing, Micko."

Detective Crew stepped onto the deck of the harbor unit named the *Detective Luis Lopez*. All NYPD harbor boats are named after fallen police heroes. Crew waved to Micko and yelled, "Good luck with your investigation."

"Thanks. I'll need it."

Eddie Dolan drove the ferry to the Hart Island dock, where the five prisoners and three corrections guards were waiting patiently to be taken back to Rikers Island. They were all on the wooden deck of the pier when Micko said, "I have to interview each of you before you step onto the ferry."

There was a lot of complaining, but Micko folded his arms and said, "This can go fast or slow. I don't care. I'm on overtime."

It didn't take long for Micko to figure out that the five cons were only at the baby cemetery while those in the other van were digging at the adult burial grounds. He also learned that the DOC guards were at the children's plots.

Micko was interested in Manny Santiago, who was nervous during the interview. He was sweating profusely, stammered when answering questions, and would not look Micko in the eye.

Micko tried to calm the nervous man by saying, "Take me to the adult cemetery."

Micko and Manny climbed into van one and soon pulled up to section 440C.

"This is where they were digging, but because of the wet ground, the backhoe could not dig deep enough without the walls collapsing," Manny said. "That's why Andy radioed the ferry—so they could get back to Rikers and change clothes and clean up."

Micko slowly took in the scene and walked around the burial plots. There was obvious evidence of digging as well as collapses. Something just didn't look right. Micko couldn't figure out what it was, so he used his cell phone to snap several pictures of section 440C.

Soon they were all aboard the *Ichabod's Crane* headed back to City Island. The DOC investigators, under the supervision of Inspector General Tom Sullivan, would conduct preliminary interviews before taking the entire DOC crew back to Rikers Island Prison for further questioning.

Although this incident was being treated as an accident, five people were dead and heads had to roll after a full investigation. The Department of Corrections would be thorough in the accident investigation, but Micko would be more thorough in his.

* * *

Inspector General Tom Sullivan had his team of investigators combing Hart Island for clues. The Department of Corrections was eager to close this case as an unfortunate accident.

The IG intentionally sent his men to investigate insignificant areas of the landmass. Tom Sullivan was clever and immediately saw suspicious evidence near the adult grave site.

"Chris, take a team up to the children's cemetery. Jocko, take another team and search the pier area," he said.

When his men were out of sight, Sullivan examined grave site 440C. He had remarkable investigative skills and quickly deduced what had happened. Cons dig, cons find something, and cons hide something.

The IG followed the muddy tire tracks to a collapsing red-brick building. One quick look, and he knew the found property had been removed from this building and taken somewhere else.

Chapter 6

It was dark when Micko got back to the New York Kayak Club. A reporter gave him and his dive gear a lift. He was too tired to clean his gear there, so he stored it in his car to be cleaned at home.

Micko lived in a quiet neighborhood nearby, so the drive was short. He grabbed his dive gear and gathered his paperwork so he could type up his reports while the information was fresh in his mind.

The first thing Micko did was to rub Mr. McGillicudy's belly and feed him. He then fed himself. He kicked himself in the ass for giving the lobsters and clams to Bill Gerhard.

After eating a hamburger and french fries, Micko took some time to put his notes in chronological order as required for a typed report.

Micko took a quick shower to clean up as well as clear his head for a long night of typing. DD5s were required during all investigations. It was well after midnight when he sat back in his chair to take a break. His cat was smart enough to go to sleep hours earlier. Micko often talked out loud when trying to make sense of his investigations, and his dutiful cat usually sat nearby and pretended to care.

This silliness was comforting to the overworked detective. Wives would nag, dogs would bark, but a cat just purred a comforting tune. Silly or not, this helped him a great deal.

Micko made another cup of coffee. Something was nagging at him, but he couldn't figure out what it was.

"Wake up, Mr. McGillicudy. What's wrong with this picture?"

The sleepy cat woke up and jumped onto Micko's computer desk to rub his face into that of his master. The cat brushed against Micko's cell phone, and it fell to the floor.

"Mac, you have to be more careful. This is an expensive—"

He stopped in midsentence. "You adorable cat. I should call you Sherlock." Micko grabbed the phone, downloaded the cemetery photos to his computer, and enlarged them.

It hit him immediately. The backhoe placed the dug-up dirt on the ridge of the grave hole like a dirt border to be replaced after the pine coffins were lowered, except a large swath of dirt was missing.

"Why is that dirt missing, and where did it go?" he asked his cat.

Dead tired but energized, he stared at the other pictures. It suddenly became clear to him. It was difficult to make out, but in the background of one photo was a set of muddy tire tracks heading toward some abandoned buildings.

Micko walked around his apartment and spoke out loud to Mac as he tried to make sense of this discrepancy. *Why did the backhoe pick up dirt and take it to an abandoned building?*

Suddenly Micko remembered the coin he found in the van. He ran to the other room and frantically searched his scuba vest pocket. There it was. In the chaos of the spinning water in the van, he thought it might be a good-luck coin or a religious medal belonging to one of the prisoners. Now he could see that it was an unusually shaped large silver coin. The markings were unclear, so Micko poured out a small amount of vinegar and cleaned the coin until the dirt dissolved.

Fifteen minutes later, Micko was scrutinizing the coin with a magnifying glass, and a smile crossed his face. He was holding a silver coin with the date 1622 stamped on it. On the other side was the slight outline of a number eight.

Details were worn away, but it was obviously an ancient coin called a piece of eight. Micko used the Google search engine to investigate this coin, which was about the size of an American silver dollar.

It didn't take long for Micko to learn about pieces of eight. They were first cast in 1497 by the Spanish and for centuries were considered the international form of currency. The Spanish used high-grade silver, and each piece weighed one ounce. The edges of coins were irregular. If the coins weighed too much, then a small piece would be cut off the edges to round out the proper weight. These small pieces would be melted into the next coin to be processed.

The large pieces of eight were called eight reals. These were worth a lot of money, so the real eight was often cut into eight pieces of lower denomination—thus the phrase "pieces of eight."

Reals that were made of gold were called doubloons and were cast similarly to the silver reals, only they were worth much more.

Micko was holding a solid piece of eight, and suddenly visions of piracy came to mind. *Could those cons have dug a burial pit and inadvertently uncovered a pirate treasure?*

This would account for the appearance of dirt being picked up and moved to hide something. If a treasure chest was indeed found, then it would be worth millions of dollars. That was a great motive for murder.

Micko had to race over to Hart Island to check out his theory. It was almost two o'clock in the morning, but he had to press on.

Chapter 7

Mundo assembled his small group of gang members, and they climbed into the stolen black Cadillac Escalade. They brought shovels and a large industrial tarp. The plan was to drive to City Island and drop off two of the gang members at a marina. The Escalade would then drive the remaining three to a dead-end street at the south end of the island and wait for the two to steal a boat and pick them up.

The posse of thieves would then ride to the east side of Hart Island, beach the stolen boat, locate the correct red-brick building, and dig the crumbling chest out of the dirt mound.

Since they already knew the chest was rotting and collapsing, they intended to place it in the tarpaulin and use two poles to carry the treasure back to the boat. Two men at each end of the net with the poles resting on their shoulders could gently transport the booty. Mundo was silently congratulating himself for his brilliant plan.

* * *

Lynch Turner called J. K. Kevins and Waldo Wellington to do the job. J. K. was a boater with considerable experience. Waldo was a gunman who also had considerable experience.

The two Irishmen went to Paddy's on the Bay Restaurant and marina, where J. K. moored his boat, the *Emerald Isle*. This was a quick, sporty, dual-console Pro-Line 23 cabin cruiser.

JK quickly fired up the twin outboards.

"Do you think Lynch was drunk when he told you about this treasure?" Waldo asked.

"No, he was dead serious and dead sober," J. K. said. After a minute, he added, "Lynch said we must be careful because another armed team may also come out tonight after the treasure."

Waldo nodded his head as he subconsciously felt for his nine-millimeter pistol wedged into his shoulder holster.

The *Emerald Isle* was moored in a section of water between the Throgs Neck Bridge and the Whitestone Bridge. J. K. expertly maneuvered his boat eastward five miles until he reached the southern tip of Hart Island. He rode past the island, turned left, and drove halfway up the other side until he reached a small beach.

A sudden thunderstorm struck just as the duo were beaching their boat.

"Push it up higher on the beach. The tide is coming in, and we don't want to come back and find the boat floating away," J. K. bellowed to Waldo over the howl of the wind.

The men grabbed their shovels and canvas bags and walked along a short patch of sand until they reached a small grassy plain. From here, they walked twenty yards until they reached a rugged path surrounded by grave markers.

Through the storm, J. K. yelled, "We go right until we reach the third dilapidated red-brick building."

The men had difficulty seeing in the dark, especially with the rain blowing into their eyes. They had been instructed not to splay their flashlights until after they had entered the remains of the Phoenix House.

They walked slowly on the uneven path until Waldo said, "JK, there's a trail of muddy clumps from a construction vehicle over here. Lynch said they used one to transport the loot. Let's follow it."

Waldo and J. K. followed the dirt trail, which led to a collapsing building. J. K. turned on his flashlight and trained it on the facade. It was the Phoenix House. With a smile, he said to his buddy, "We're halfway there."

* * *

Micko could hardly contain his excitement as he drove up to Gerhard's Marina. He quickly identified himself to the night watchman, Tim Collins, who was a drinking buddy in a local pub. Collins opened the gate and said, "It's pretty late to head out with a storm coming, don't you think?"

"A what coming?"

Just as he asked, the skies opened and the wind picked up.

"Thanks for putting the whammy on me, Tim," Micko joked.

Micko made his way down the piers until he reached *Master Baiter* docked near the end. This was Bill Gerhard's fishing boat. At thirty-five feet, this express fisherman boat Albemarle 288 was built for speed and offshore fishing. This craft was too large to keep berthed in his small marina.

The keys were always in the same spot, under the weathered brown pilot-seat cushion. The waves were kicking up, and the docked boat rocked and rolled in its berth.

Micko knew how to pilot a boat, but he was still a novice. The weather made him a bit uneasy, but his excitement got the better of him. It had been a long day, and the conditions were unstable. But he had to know. *Is there buried treasure hiding on Hart Island?*

* * *

The two Outlaws exited the Escalade in front of the Pelican Marina. The entrance gate was locked, and a guard dog barked as they climbed the fence.

"Quiet down, Duke, you'll wake all the neighbors," the security guard warned. "It's probably that damn raccoon again."

The guard shined his flashlight in tight arcs as he walked toward the gate. When he was assured that the gate was still locked and nobody was messing with it, he walked back toward the marina office to finish his coffee.

Shielding his eyes against the cutting wind and rain, he never saw the hooded figure spring out of the shadows and grab him in a bear hug from behind. Before he could react, a sharp blade cut deep into his neck, severing his jugular. He gurgled on his own warm blood. As he lost consciousness, his last thought was, *Duke, you were right.*

The guard dog was tethered to a post outside the main office. The dead watchman was dragged under a boat-repair scaffolding, and the men gave the vicious dog a wide berth as they entered the office.

While the dog's incessant barking was muffled by the increasing wind, the killers ransacked the office until they came upon a set of boat keys with a name tag attached.

The two gang members raced down the docks, desperately searching for the boat matching the keys. All of a sudden, it was dancing in the rough water right in front of them—a sleek bright orange and yellow high-performance boat named *Speedy Gonzalez.*

The men quickly jumped on board and started the huge engines.

"This mutherfucka be fast, but there ain't room fo' all o' us," one Outlaw said to the other.

* * *

Micko drove Bill's boat at a reasonable speed. He knew the waters well from years of kayaking the area, but the rough waves made him cautious. He was glad this type of fishing vessel had an overhead covering and full windshield as he watched the rain streaming down.

There was no time to call Bill and ask permission to use the boat, and he certainly would not call at this ungodly hour. Micko took it slow as he made his approach to Hart Island.

* * *

Mundo and his men were huddled in the dry confines of the Cadillac when they heard the loud engines approach from the sea.

"What da hell be dat?" he screeched at the two men in the speedboat.

Both yelled back unintelligibly as the wind swept away their words.

Mundo hurried his remaining men on board and took over the controls. There were two seats up front and a small bench seat in the rear. Three gangsters had to cramp onto the rear bench seat as Mundo pulled into the Long Island Sound.

"Two o' yo' gonna have ta stay on tha island while we take tha crap back ta tha Cadillac," he said angrily. "Then we gotta have ta come back fo' yo'. Tha stupid boat thieves gotta stay behind."

With that, he gunned the boat and started racing toward Hart Island but quickly realized the speedboat was severely overweight. The waves pounded the boat hard, and *Speedy Gonzalez* was downshifted so it wasn't too speedy.

Mundo fought hard to keep control of the boat. He had little experience with boating, and the sleek hull of this craft was giving him fits with poor stability.

As *Speedy Gonzalez* erratically rolled through the whitecaps, the Black Outlaws vomited on one another in a wave of seasickness. Several shovels got pitched overboard by the rough seas and overcrowded conditions.

Mundo decided to try sprinting the skinny boat through the breakers and found that the extra speed was giving him more stability. They arrived at their destination in fifteen minutes.

Chapter 8

J.K. and Waldo raced into the comfort of the ancient building. Even though it was crumbling, it afforded relief from the deteriorating conditions outside.

The two shined their flashlights silently inside this cave-like dwelling until the lights struck the pile of dirt Lynch had told them to find. A sinking feeling came over them.

There was a large disturbance in the dirt pile. Something had been removed.

"We're too freaking late," Waldo said.

"Let's get out of here quick," J. K. said.

* * *

Mundo was getting used to piloting the speedboat when they approached the east side of Hart Island and noticed another boat beached there.

Mundo quickly ran *Speedy Gonzalez* up onto the sand and directed his two boat thieves, "Stay wit' *Speedy Gonzalez* until we git back. Guard her asshole wit' yo' goddamn lives. Tha rest o' yo' guys, check yo' goddamn guns. Itz go time!"

* * *

The two Irish Mafia goons were walking quickly with their heads bowed into the blowing wind. They wanted to get into their boat and race away as fast as possible.

Suddenly, Waldo shouted, "Hello." He bent down and picked up a shiny object from a puddle.

"JK, I found a piece of gold!"

"Let me look at that," J. K. said. "This sure as shit is an old coin. It must have fallen out of the chest when it was moved. Look around this trail. There may be more."

The two kicked their feet through puddles and shined their lights back and forth across the roadway on the way back to the *Emerald Isle*. They were disappointed not to find any more coins but were much more disappointed when Mundo's men opened fire on them.

The strong smell of cordite quickly blew away as the crooks reloaded.

"Stop! Stop, yo' fools! We need 'em alive in case they found da loot 'n' rehid dat shit," Mundo screamed above the howling wind.

A quick examination of the two men sprawled on the lawn confirmed Mundo's fear. They were dead.

"Bubba, git back 'n' git dem two niggas on da beach, then take dem dead guys 'n' place 'em in their muthafuckin' boat. We'll open da throttle 'n' push 'em out ta sea. I don't want their muthafuckin' bodies found anywhere nea' here," Mundo barked.

Mundo continued to the Phoenix House and discovered the disturbed dirt pile. He furtively swung his flashlight all over the massive room.

"Where did dem two pricks move da chest ta?" he roared.

There was no visible trace inside the collapsing building, and he knew a search outdoors in the weather conditions would be fruitless.

"Back ta tha boat. We'll have ta come back on a cleara night. Whoeva dem dead guys were workin' fo' don't have a clue where the fuck tha loot be eitha. Dat gotta be a desperate race ta find dat shit."

When Mundo and his gangsters arrived back at the beach, the dead men were already propped up in the *Emerald Isle*.

Then Mundo had a better idea. "No, take dem dead bastards down 'n' place 'em in *Speedy Gonzalez*. Dis boat be too hot since yo' idiots killed da security guard. Let tha cops blame dem guys fo' tha murda 'n' boat theft, 'n' let 'em believe they were killed ova a drug deal gone shizzle.

"Bubba, tie a bungee cord ta tha steerin' wheel 'n' then open tha throttle," Mundo ordered.

Bubba jumped into the cockpit of *Speedy Gonzalez* as the others pushed her off the sand. Once the boat was in deeper water, Bubba started the massive engines and turned her facing due east. He used the bungee cord to secure the straightened wheel to the pilot seat.

He looked around nervously before pushing the throttle all the way forward. As the boat raced off, Bubba jumped out and floundered in the water until the crew of the *Emerald Isle* cruised up and dragged him aboard.

Mundo hoped *Speedy Gonzalez* would cross the channel between Hart Island and the Queens County mainland and travel the forty or so miles to the Long Island North Shore. The authorities would never know where the dead Irishmen had been shot, and he and his men could come back and search for the treasure the next night.

The *Emerald Isle* was just racing out of the beach area, and Mundo turned south to retrace his route back to the Escalade. He was unfamiliar with boating and water directions. He just knew to follow the directions that Manny had given him.

So far, so good. I can do this again tomorrow night, he thought.

Suddenly, a boat appeared heading for them from the southern tip of Hart Island.

"Jesus, Mundo, dat shit must be tha cops!" one of the henchmen wailed. "Someone must have heard tha gunshots 'n' called 'em."

Mundo immediately turned the boat 180 degrees and headed north. His mind was racing, and he thought, *maybe I can lose them in the darkness under cover of this rain.*

His intentions were to run up the north end of Hart Island, then turn left and head south along the west end of the island to avoid the police. He would then be heading toward the south end of City Island, where his escape vehicle was parked.

Mundo raced the *Emerald Isle* as fast as she would go. Although he was riding into unfamiliar waters, he knew he was near the end of the island when he heard the incessant clanging of a warning buoy.

When the bell sounded close, Mundo turned the boat left. The deep darkness of the night, combined with the blinding rain, allowed Mundo to only guess where he was going.

Mundo turned the boat too hard at a dangerous rate of speed. A rogue wave caught the *Emerald Isle* broadside just as she pitched high on the crest of a wave.

The boat felt like she had been rammed by another one. The cruiser leaned precariously to the left, and three of the Outlaws were thrown overboard. Mundo and Bubba were thrown to the deck.

Mundo quickly jumped back to his feet and tried to wrestle with the steering wheel to gain control.

"Mundo, dat gang got throwed overboard!" Bubba screamed over the intense wind.

"It's naw every thug fo' his dirty ass. I can't control dis boat ta git back fo' 'em," Mundo said.

Even though he had the boat's throttle opened to the max, the wind and waves controlled his flight. He was riding blind until he saw a familiar sight.

"Bubba, I know where we at. Dat's Orchard Beach straight ahead," he said.

Mundo raced the *Emerald Isle* straight up the beach at top speed. The two men were flung forward like two puppets. When they regained their composure, Mundo took off at a full sprint up the beachhead to the boardwalk. He ran left toward the main concourse and concession stands. Bubba was right on his heels.

* * *

Micko piloted his boat at a reasonable speed and turned the corner to the east side of Hart Island. He was proceeding cautiously when he saw two boats in the distance. One was racing away from the island, and Micko could tell by the sound of the engine that it was a high-performance speedboat.

The other boat, a fishing-style vessel, was coming in his direction from the area of the beach. Suddenly, the fishing boat made a U-turn and headed north at a rapid pace.

Micko found this to be disturbing. Two boats out on a night like this, around Hart Island at three in the morning. Both boats appeared to be running away from something.

In a matter of minutes, Micko pulled the *Master Baiter* up to the small beach and immediately noticed the distinct marks of two boats. Even in the black of night with the teeming rain, the two straight grooves in the sand easily gave away the other boats' visits.

Micko grabbed his high-intensity flashlight and took off for grave section 440C. He crossed the grassy knoll, and his flashlight reflected off several shiny objects glistening in the rain. He bent down and picked up three of them. Bullet shells, still warm.

Micko went into defense mode. He turned off his light and pulled his gun. He slowly approached the muddy trail and let his eyes adjust to the darkness.

He listened intently but could hear only the blustering wind and pouring rain. The muddy tracks he had seen in the pictures were washed away. Micko was reluctant to turn his flashlight back on, but he had come this far, so he continued.

He walked toward the row of ramshackle red-brick buildings. He shined his light into the lobby area of the first two and saw dusty cobweb-infested rooms in the two-story buildings.

The third was a three-story building in far worse shape than the other two. Upon shining his light, Micko immediately saw evidence of recent activity.

The front door was missing, and the entrance led into a cavernous room. Walls had been knocked down and furniture removed. Micko had no idea what this house was used for, but he noticed muddy tracks on the floor.

The tracks led to a murky pile of dirt. Two obviously unused shovels lay nearby. The dirt mound showed signs of being disturbed, but not by these shovels.

On closer examination, Micko realized that whatever was once buried in that dirt had been removed. He also observed several sets of muddy boot prints. They went in all directions, as if the people wearing the boots were searching for something.

Micko sat against a wall deep in thought. He often did this at scenes of homicides he was assigned to investigate. He would think for hours like this. If a question came to mind, he would address it at the scene of the crime, not from his desk at the detective squad.

The confused detective sat and rehearsed in his mind what may have happened. He comically wished he had Mr. McGillicudy there to listen as he talked over his theories.

Convicts are digging graves when they stumble upon a treasure. With the help of the corrections officers, they move the treasure and hide it here. Heavy rain comes, and two boats arrive. Obviously, they are both looking for the treasure. They have beached boats here and left shovels and footprints.

But what happened to the treasure? It appears there is not much of a mess at the dirt mound area. How was it moved? Clean shovels indicate the boat people probably didn't get it. That would mean the treasure might have been moved prior to their arrival. Then again, maybe one group removed the treasure in a fashion that I just can't think of. There are no heavy tracks or drag marks in the room or in the mud trail. How was it moved, and who was shooting at whom?

Micko rubbed his weary eyes and realized how tired he was. Sitting there could do him no good, so he went home to get a few hours of sleep. The sun would be rising soon, and he still had lots of work to do. Reports had to be typed, investigations and interviews had to be conducted, and he had to update the chief of detectives.

* * *

Mundo and Bubba sat in a dry cove behind the Orchard Beach concession stands. They were thanking their lucky stars for being alive and thinking about their next course of action.

"Bubba, let's git next door ta where the fuck tha Parks Department keeps their muthafuckin' vehicles. I know a thug who the fuck once worked here as a summa provision job. Dude says dat dem guys take turns usin' tha cars 'n' trucks, so they keep tha keys inside tha cabs."

In the second GMC truck, Bubba found the keys above the sun visor. Within minutes, the two were driving home to their warm beds. When they were away from the High Island antenna, Mundo called Maria and gave her the bad news. Maria then called Manny.

Manny immediately knew he had been betrayed by Andy, just as he tried to betray Andy. Andy's men got there first, must have seen Mundo and his gang arrive, and hid the treasure again. Dead men tell no tales, so Manny didn't know where the treasure was now. Since the High Island radio antenna interfered with cell phone use, it was a good bet that Andy didn't know where the treasure had been moved to either.

Chapter 9

Flat Nose Freddie was busy in the makeshift lab he built deep inside the missile silo. Here he processed his heroin brand, which was of distinctly purer product.

At first glance, the strange beakers and tubing looked chaotic, but Freddie had everything well under control. He was aware of the dangers involved with the combustible substances that he used, and he took all the necessary precautions.

The only factor he had no control over was the ventilation of the deadly, flammable fumes produced during the heroin purification process. He had an exhaust system built into the lab walls, but the fumes had to travel fifty feet to an escape hole outside the silo.

This exhaust could be spotted by the grave diggers, so Freddie had to go outdoors to ensure that nobody was in view of the smoke cloud. This was not a problem most days because his entrance to the silo was near the children's cemetery, and no one ever went there except for an occasional burial.

Freddie walked from the lab up three stories to his main shelter and living quarters. In his office, several screens offered him a 180-degree view outside his compound, courtesy of an expensive video system. The cameras automatically went into night vision after sunset.

All looked clear, so Freddie turned on the lab's exhaust fan and decided to go outdoors for some fresh air. He walked along a long, well-lit corridor to the steel rung ladder that led to the surface.

In years past, this burrow was used as a supply drop. Missile fuel, parts, and other equipment were lowered by a hand-cranked pulley to the mini loading dock. Then the products were placed onto pallets and wheeled by carts to the required workplaces.

He slowly opened the heavy metal turret cover and quickly sucked in the fresh salty air. Freddie decided to stretch his legs a bit and walked into the thicket behind his silo opening.

He watched as the ferryboat approached from City Island. He knew the prisoners' and guards' routines, so he felt safe sitting on the small bluff over-looking the water. He knew they would take their time loading their digging tools and deciding what site they would work at for the day.

Freddie watched as the vans approached a large dig site. After off-loading coffins, the box truck and one van drove to where he was sitting.

Shit, they must have some baby coffins to bury, he thought.

Freddie crawled into the thickest part of the weeds and watched as the truck and van drove past him and stopped at the children's cemetery. He watched them unload the tiny coffins, and one con fired up the small Bobcat to cover the graves. The van and driver then returned to the adult section while the prisoners on burial detail had lunch.

Stuck out in the open was the last place Freddie wanted to be, so he moved along the underbrush to a spot midway between the two grave sites. He knew the mobile guards would stay at the baby graves, so he crept closer to the adult cemetery.

The wind was blowing north, so he could hear the conversations among the prisoners and the corrections officers. He laughed to himself when he saw the muddy walls of the dig fall in upon itself. He didn't laugh when they excitedly dug up an object.

Freddie couldn't see what it was, but it caused quite a stir among the guards and cons. A heated exchange ended when the backhoe picked up the object in a front loader full of mud and drove it to an abandoned building.

He watched as one van drove back to the children's graves, and the driver acted natural, as if nothing had happened. The other van drove all the prisoners back to the ferry. Freddie could see that the two corrections officers and the cons were keeping this secret to themselves.

Since the group of prisoners and guards stayed at the baby graveyard, Freddie was stuck out in the open. He was sure that nobody could see the exhaust, which had since turned almost invisible as the lab was aired out.

He moved back to his sitting spot near the water's edge and was watching the ferry depart when he observed the prisoner van sprint in reverse and plunge off the rear of the *Ichabod's Crane*.

Freddie immediately knew that whatever the cons had dug up was extremely valuable. This was not an accident. The corrections officer in charge of those prisoners had just murdered them to keep them quiet.

Before long, the other van left the children's cemetery and went to the ferry dock. Freddie watched all the activity from the safety of his waterside perch while the burial detail watched from the ferry dock a half-mile away.

When the harbor unit divers entered the water, Freddie ran to the Bobcat. He knew the keys were always inside and that all eyes and ears would be watching as the divers pulled up the sunken van.

Freddie awkwardly maneuvered the Bobcat into the Phoenix House and dug into the middle of the dirt mound. He was astonished that the heavy chest came out on his first scoop.

He quickly carried the mud and its precious cargo to the loading tunnel of his silo. He stopped the vehicle and inspected the mud-covered cargo. He could see how fragile the chest was, so he climbed down the rusty ladder rungs to the loading dock below.

He removed a webbed cargo net, attached it to the end of the loading crane, and cranked it to the surface. Then he climbed to the top of the silo entrance and spread the net on the ground.

Within minutes, he had the muddy chest lying in the middle of the net. The front loader easily lowered its cargo into place.

The miniature crane had a topside lever as well as one below. Freddie cranked the trunk off the ground, over the tunnel entrance, and down to the loading dock.

Freddie climbed back down the ladder and moved a flatbed pallet under the cargo. A few quick cranks, and the precious load was on the flatbed and wheeled to a special underground utility room.

He grabbed a small shovel and climbed back to the surface. The cargo net had lifted the treasure chest but not the mud. The mud was a dead giveaway to his hideout, so Freddie shoveled the mud mountain into the thicket.

When he was certain his theft could not be traced, he drove the Bobcat back to its original location and climbed back into the silo to investigate his booty.

Chapter 10

It felt like Micko's head had just hit the pillow when the phone rang.

"All right, Detective, since I haven't gotten any written reports from you, give me a verbal account of your progress."

The COD sounded pissed. Micko quickly ran through the night's events and his theories for Chief Clifford. There was a long silence before Clifford said, "There might be some merit to your theories, O'Shaughnessy."

Micko listened intently as his chief updated him on events.

While Micko was catching a few hours of sleep, a security guard at the Pelican Marina was found murdered and a speedboat was reported stolen. The boat was found wrecked along Halfmoon Beach in Port Washington, Queens, with two dead men aboard. They were both shot multiple times.

At the same time, another boat was found washed up on the sand at Orchard Beach in the Bronx. There were no bodies aboard, but the coast guard found three DOA floaters just offshore.

Micko was stunned.

"Chief, run the registrations of those boats and the pedigree of the dead men, along with known associates," Micko said. He knew the chief was being proactive on this case and was probably loving every minute of it.

"It's already been done, and the info is being sent to your cell phone. I'll cut you some slack on your lack of reports if you continue the good work."

Micko sat up on his bed trying to absorb all the chief had told him. Mr. McGillicudy was lying next to him, fast asleep.

The alarm clock showed it was nine o'clock, well past his cat's feeding time. Mac was not allowed to sleep on the bed, but he probably tired from trying to wake his master.

Micko's thoughts raced wildly as he petted his loyal companion. His cell phone beeped, and the information the chief had promised arrived. Before he would dig into this new info, the cat had to be fed, and the coffee had to be made.

Reading slowly through the information, Micko learned that the two dead men on the speedboat were Irish Mafia. The owner of the stolen speedboat was a prominent Bronx businessman who was probably just a larceny victim here.

The boat found washed up on Orchard Beach had not been reported stolen. Micko blew past the boat's registration info until something caught his eye. The registered owner of the *Emerald Isle* was J. K. Kevins, one of the dead Irish.

What the hell is Kevins doing on a stolen boat in Queens while his own boat is beached in the Bronx? This doesn't make any sense, he thought.

Micko knew he was reaching, but he decided to call the Forty-Fifth Precinct and speak with the detective catching the homicide of the marina security guard.

Detective Jack Cusack was put on the phone. "Hello, Micko, what can I do you for?"

"Hi, Jack. What can you tell me about that guard who was killed last night?"

"It looks like someone sneaked up behind him, grabbed him from the rear, and sliced his throat from ear to ear. The marina's offices were ransacked, but it seems that only the keys to a speedboat were taken. The surveillance cameras show two shadowy figures. Very poor clarity because of the weather, but they look like a Laurel and Hardy couple. One big guy and one little guy. The big guy was the butcher."

"Thanks, Jack. I owe you a beer."

"That's what you said last time I did you a favor, O'Shaughnessy. By the way, we recovered a stolen vehicle a few blocks away from the crime scene. It's being dusted for prints right now."

"Jack, do me another favor, and I'll owe you big time. Compare the prints on that vehicle to those floaters found near Orchard Beach."

* * *

"You betrayed me, Manny!" Andy yelled into his phone.

"We betrayed each other," Manny said. "I waited for you at Hurley's bar but found out the cops had you for most of the night. After the van fell off the barge, I had to make a quick decision about the fate of the treasure."

Andy thought about this for a moment and asked, "So what do you propose?"

"We go back to work as usual and try to relocate the treasure ourselves, together. I think your guys moved it to a more secure location. But neither of us knows where that is," Manny answered.

The horrific fate of Andy's pals was all over the news. Manny was right. Andy had no idea where Lynch's cohorts had relocated the treasure. He guessed that the weather was so severe that they had no other choice. Then Manny's men killed them before anyone learned about the new hiding spot.

"Why don't we meet today and try to figure this out? How about Hurley's?" Manny asked.

"All right, I'll meet you there later," Andy said. Anything was better than staying at home with his incessantly nagging wife.

* * *

Micko spent the early part of the day fielding a number of phone calls. He learned that the three dead men found floating near Orchard Beach were part of the notorious Black Outlaws gang. Their fingerprints were inside the stolen Escalade recovered near the Pelican Marina murder scene.

Two of the dead men matched the description of the Laurel and Hardy murderers of the security guard. Other fingerprints recovered from the stolen Cadillac belonged to other Outlaws gang members.

Chief of Detectives Clifford had a team of intelligence specialists connecting the dots. Prints from Mundo, the leader of the Outlaws, were lifted from the stolen car. A check of his known associates discovered that he once ran with Maria, Manny Santiago's current squeeze. This connected Manny indirectly to the Outlaws.

Micko made a call to the Queens County morgue. "Hey, Duff, what's happening?"

Dick Duffy was the detective assigned to the county morgue.

"Not much, Micko. What do you need?"

"Those two guys in the speedboat who were all shot up—has the autopsy been performed yet?" Micko asked.

"Yeah, Doc Habib just finished."

"Duff, I need to know the caliber of the bullets and what personal items they were carrying," Micko said.

"They were shot multiple times with a nine-millimeter and three eighty slugs. They were carrying only a cell phone, car and house keys, and a weird coin. No wallets or cash."

"So they were shot by at least two shooters. Duff, can you get those slugs to the lab and see if they came from two guns or several guns? Thanks, pal."

He was just about to hang up when he said, "Strange coin. What do you mean, strange coin?"

"I don't know. It's a dirty gold coin about the size of an American silver dollar. It's old. That's all I can tell you about it."

"Dick, send it to the Fifty-Second Squad forthwith," Micko said excitedly.

The next phone call came from one of Chief Clifford's specialists.

"Detective O'Shaughnessy?"

"Yes, what do you have?"

"One of those dead Irish mobsters has ties with a guy who works in Rikers Island Prison named William Turner. They have a record of getting arrested together for petty crimes."

"Holy shit! Do me a favor and see if there is any connection between Turner and Andy Hastings, who is also a guard in Rikers," Micko said.

"Oh, there is. They play cards together a few times a month, and they vacationed together in Dublin with their wives."

That's it, that's it. This is all starting to come together, Micko thought.

He sat back in his chair and was in deep thought when his partner interrupted. "Micko, you look like you need some sleep."

Micko opened his eyes and looked warmly at Gus Lopez. They had been partners for years, but now Chief Clifford had him working alone on this case and poor Gus had his workload doubled. Gus looked like *he* needed a good sleep.

"Gus, I'm almost done with this case, and we'll be working together real soon." Micko laughed.

"Yeah, that's what you said when you flew off to the South Pacific the first time. Then you bring me there for your second caper and get me into a shootout and get my arm busted." Gus grinned.

"Let me run this by you before I type up my reports for COD Clifford."

Micko took his time to explain to his partner how he thought a gang of five prisoners and two guards accidentally stumbled upon a buried treasure. Immediately, avarice, murder, and betrayal took its toll on the cons. There were now five dead convicts so the two remaining guards could split the booty between themselves. But they betrayed each other by sending cohorts to retrieve the treasure, and more murders occurred.

He continued. Andy Hastings was stuck being interviewed most of the night, so he called his Rikers pal, William Turner. Turner was stuck on shift, so he called his Irish pals to dig up the chest. At the same time, Manny Santiago had his girlfriend call members of the Black Outlaws mob to dig up the trunk. The two groups met, and a furious shootout ensued, leaving the two Irishmen dead and the treasure location unknown.

Gus looked incredulously at his partner. "Treasure? Where do you get this idea of treasure?"

Micko pulled the piece of eight out of his pocket. "Gus, I found this in the sunken van. It must have been found by one of the inmates. It was the only thing on them. Plus, one of the dead Irishmen had a strange gold piece in his pocket. The only connection is that they were both on Hart Island. I'm betting that the gold coin is a Spanish doubloon."

As Gus walked away laughing, Micko dutifully sat at his computer and began his reports.

Soon an impish little courier entered the 52 Squad and asked, "Is there a Detective Micko here?"

"It's Detective O'Shaughnessy, shorty. Now let me sign for that."

Micko opened the small manila envelope, and a gold coin slipped out. He studied it carefully, then took it to the washroom for a good cleaning. When it was sufficiently cleaned, he peered at the brilliant coin through a strong magnifying glass. The engravings were well worn down, but he could make out the date: 1607.

Thanks, Duffy. He grinned slyly.

Gus was visibly amazed and said, "Micko, you should go to the library and check that out."

Micko thought for a moment and realized his pal was right. He would go to the City Island Library and research Hart Island, Spanish treasure, local pirates, and gold doubloons. Libraries contained ancient manuscripts and information that could not be found doing Google searches.

Chapter 11

"What the hell happened out there, you bastard?"

Andy knew that Turner was furious. "Sorry, Lynch. It was a cluster-fuck. I betrayed Manny, and he in turn deceived me."

"Do you know what kind of position you put me in with the Irish Patriots? My head is on the chopping block. The Patriots need reparation to ensure loyalty. I'm a walking dead man!" Lynch screamed.

"Listen, Lynch, I'll bet my life that they kept the treasure a secret from the Patriots," Andy said. "Avarice is what got us into this mess in the first place, and I know those two ignorant pricks were as greedy as us. As far as the Irish Patriots know, they went out on their own on a mission that failed."

"I sure as shit hope you are right, Andy. Now what are we going to do about the treasure?"

"I'm meeting with Manny in a few minutes, and we'll try to work something out together. At this point, we have no choice but to trust each other or lose the loot. The inspector general is conducting a full investigation into the van incident, so the burials are suspended for now. When the investigators leave Hart Island, we can sneak out there in daylight and search for the booty."

This seemed to satisfy Lynch. He knew that J. K. and Waldo had an insatiable desire for wealth and probably never informed the Patriots of their plans.

This let him off the hook with the Irish, but he wanted reparations from the Outlaws for killing his men. Dark thoughts plagued his mind.

* * *

Micko was putting on his jacket when Gus yelled, "Micko, this call is for you."

"Detective—" Micko began.

"Damn it, I know who you are," yelled an obviously annoyed Chief Clifford. "Where are my reports on your progress?"

Micko rolled his eyes to the ceiling and briefly brought the COD up to date, explaining his theory like he explained to Gus.

Chief Clifford seemed pleased. "TARU was able to dry out the recovered cell phones and download a record of recent activity. It clearly shows phone calls from each set of DOAs directly to guards Hastings and Santiago. There is enough evidence to reclassify the drowned inmates as homicide victims, not accident victims."

Micko knew that the NYPD Technical Assistance Research Unit was the best in the world. He already had the researchers enhancing the poor-quality images from the security guard's murder. He hoped TARU could clean up the faces of the killers so he could pin the death on the Laurel and Hardy floaters from Orchard Beach.

The verbal exchange between detective and chief was brief but enlightening to both parties. Andy and Manny found something on Hart Island, and each betrayed the other by sending out armed recovery teams to gather the booty after Andy intentionally sank the prisoner van. Prisoners were murdered. The Irish mobsters were murdered. The innocent security guard was murdered.

One part of their exchange bothered Micko.

"Don't send any of your DD5 reports to that IG Sullivan," the chief warned. "*All* reports come to me direct."

Micko still had his jacket on when he suddenly reached for the crime-scene photos. He laid them out in order on the floor next to his desk. He studied them carefully and yelled, "Holy shit! The treasure is still there."

"What are you talking about?" Gus asked.

"Look, look! No mud. No mud in either of the recovered boats that went to Hart Island to steal the loot."

Gus looked at the boats in the crime-scene photos. The *Emerald Isle* was beached, and the interior was wet but clean. *Speedy Gonzalez* was covered in blood and a bit of sand as it sat aground on Halfmoon Beach.

"I don't get it," Gus said.

"The treasure chest was found in mud, picked up in mud, transported in mud, and again hidden in mud. If either of the gangs had located the chest and placed it into a boat, there would be massive amounts of mud."

Detective O'Shaughnessy came up with a new theory. The Irish gangsters must have found the treasure and realized the terrible weather would prevent them from removing it from the island, so they moved it to another spot before the Outlaw gangsters arrived.

He spun in his chair as he pondered, *the Outlaw guys must have ambushed the Irish where I found the spent cartridges. The Outlaws killed the Irish in a hail of bullets after they questioned them about the treasure. The bodies were placed into the speedboat that the Outlaws had stolen and set out into the open water. The Outlaws then stole JK's boat and raced away in the gale. These must have been the two boats he saw as he approached Hart Island.*

He got up out of his chair and walked around the squad room muttering to himself. His theory continued. *The* Emerald Isle *spotted him arriving in the* Master Baiter *and retreated at a high rate of speed. Somewhere between Hart Island and Orchard Beach, three of the Outlaws were thrown overboard in the rough seas and drowned. The boat then was intentionally run aground at Orchard Beach, and others made their escape.*

This seemed plausible. The treasure was still on Hart Island, and the only ones who knew where were dead. The Irish would never get phone reception on the island, especially during the squall, so they couldn't have told Andy where they moved the goods.

Micko grabbed a set of car keys and raced out the door, leaving Gus with a puzzled look on his face.

* * *

Lynch was frantic that his Irish comrades were out to get him. He knew how loyal the Irish Patriots were. Led by Paddy Connelly, the group was ruthless in its attempts to help Ireland free itself from England's tyranny.

The Irish Patriots were a splinter group of the Irish Republican Army, which had been greatly reduced since the 1998 Good Friday peace agreement. The IRA Council was still in existence, although it had a smaller role.

The Irish Patriots recruited members to help solicit funds across the United States for their fight for independence. These funds supported the purchase of weapons, advertisements, and attorneys.

Many of the Irish Patriots were sons and daughters of IRA fighters, while others were just brutal wannabes.

Lynch decided to make the call without telling Andy or Manny and just feign ignorance. "Hello, Paddy?"

"Yes."

"William Turner here."

"What do you want, Lynch?"

"Hey, I just heard about J. K. and Waldo. What the hell happened?"

"Waldo told his wife, Mary Kay, that they were going after buried treasure on Hart Island. Funny, she said you were the one to send them out on this task," Paddy growled.

The Irish Patriots knew. Lynch had to place the blame on someone else.

"Paddy, I told J. K. to let you know about this plan. I was stuck at work and had little access to make phone calls. I'm still being punished. I called J. K. in haste because I was afraid we would lose the treasure if I waited. This treasure would be a major score for our cause."

Lynch was desperate. "Besides, it was Manny's hood niggers that whacked our guys. We must attack the Outlaws to set an example."

"Tell me all you know," Paddy ordered.

* * *

Flat Nose Freddie was absolutely stunned when he opened the ancient chest. Gold and silver coins spilled onto the floor like a shimmering waterfall.

Intrigued, he began to study the old coins. Soon he was conducting website searches on his laptop to identify the coins and learn their value.

The full doubloon sold for anywhere from $2,500 to $5,000, depending on condition, year of mint, and other factors. This chest was filled with thousands of gold doubloons and silver pieces of eight. Freddie had hit the jackpot. This trove of precious metals was worth tens of millions of dollars.

Think! Think! Freddie was frantic. *How do I legally sell off these relics?*

Freddie knew he sat on a lucrative drug-distribution network, but the hazard of assassination from bitter rivals or life in prison was a stark reality. He was also sitting on a gold mine, but the legality was questionable.

He had to make plans to find wealthy coin collectors and museums that might covertly buy up large parcels of this booty. He could then move into a respectable home, sell off his drug empire, and slowly sell off his newly found gold and silver stock. There are always collectors whose desire for valuable coins outweighs their respect of the law.

Freddie received a text message: 911. His lieutenants who ran daily drug operations in the Parkchester projects were warned to contact him only in dire emergencies.

Freddie searched through his laptop and logged onto a special blog where coded messages were exchanged.

"Who knows that Washington was a spy working for the enemy. Now they have captured ALL outposts and put friends in jail with warrants out for others. Don't come home."

Freddie quickly typed back, "The Nose knows."

He knew what the post meant. Lester Washington was a new buyer who purchased large quantities of his street heroin labeled *King*. Freddie would have never made him out to be an undercover cop. Now his Parkchester enterprise was busted. It wouldn't be long before someone gave him up for the murders of his rivals.

Freddie was furious. He knew cops everywhere would be out looking for him. There would be a freeze on his accounts, and the cops would be on the lookout for his car and boat.

He was lucky that Wi-Fi service was enhanced in the proximity of High Island's radio antenna that disturbed cell phone service. Freddie relied on e-mails to contact his trusted cohort, Itchy. After few taps on Freddie's laptop keyboard, Itchy had his orders for the day.

*   *   *

Micko parked opposite the City Island Library and gathered his evidence in a black, weather-worn briefcase. He read on the door that the library was open only from 9:00 a.m. to 5:00 p.m. on Tuesdays, Wednesdays, and Fridays. *Budget cutbacks,* he thought.

The veteran detective looked lost as he stood in the reception area of the main library room.

"Can I help you?" a soft voice asked.

Micko turned to see a frumpy woman. She was in her early thirties, about five-foot-five, with mousy brown hair pulled into a tight bun atop her head. She wore glasses with a chain so they could hang around her neck. Her clothing was loose fitting and seemed comically out of style. She looked every bit the Hollywood-crafted librarian type, only younger.

"Yes, I need to borrow a few books for a week or two," he said.

"Do you have a library card?"

"A what? Oh no, I haven't been in a library since my early teens." He laughed.

"Well, I can assure you that this is not a laughing matter. This is a NYC library, and you *must* have a library card to remove any books, texts, or videos."

"Oh, that's OK. I'm an NYPD detective. See, we're on the same team." He flashed his detective shield.

"Let me take a closer look at that badge. Do you have an ID card?"

Micko produced his NYPD ID card and showed it to her as he asked, "Why? you don't believe me?"

"Detective O'Shaughnessy, you look quite disheveled. Your tie is pizza stained and loose around your neck, and your hair looks like you combed it with a pork chop. Now, why wouldn't I believe you?"

Micko suddenly realized he must be a sorry sight. He had been working long hours, and it took its toll on his overall grooming.

"I love your accent," was all he could muster in response.

"You cops are all alike." She laughed. "If you were dressed neatly, I would suspect you were an impersonator."

"Hey, I can dress pretty snazzy when I'm not working twenty hours a day," he joked back.

"OK, how can I help you?"

Micko suddenly liked this young woman. "I'm working a homicide case and need some information about Hart Island and pirate treasure."

She slowly took off her reading glasses and let them fall to her chest as she eyeballed the detective. "How do you go from investigating a murder to pirates?" she asked with a tone of doubt.

Micko saw her emerald-green eyes and was taken aback. They were mesmerizing. He was unable to come up with a covert answer. *I wonder what assets are hidden beneath those dowdy clothes,* he thought.

"Let's sit down at a table, and I'll explain."

He told her about what appeared to be an accidental death of the prisoners and the two recovered coins that may or may not be pirate booty. She listened intently, and her eyes never left his.

"My accent is from Casa del Sol, Spain, and my name is Esmeralda." She stuck out her hand.

"My friends call me Micko." He shook her hand gently.

"OK, Micko, I am going on my lunch break, so if you take me to the City Island Diner, I'll tell you all about Hart Island."

Chapter 12

Itchy was driving the *Who Nose* at a normal speed when his Droid buzzed. His boss had given him instructions via e-mail, and he was proceeding as instructed. The new message coached him to make a highly unusual and dangerous daytime delivery at Hart Island.

The usual procedure was to take packages of heroin at night to the beach area. Itchy would land the small Zodiac at a certain location and cover it with camo netting. The product would be in a waterproof knapsack, and Itchy would walk to the silo and deliver the drugs.

The first message directed Itchy to purchase a number of items that were not drug related. Then he was told to drive Freddie's boat just offshore of Hart Island and pretend to be fishing until dark.

This message directed him to drive the *Who Nose* Zodiac in shore to a small, well-covered lagoon. Once the small boat was dragged into a cove, it would be covered with pine branches. A hidden underground passageway led into the labyrinth of the abandoned missile silo system.

This was highly irregular, as was the strange request for the extra weaponry, suitcases, and waterproof Pelican cases. When Itchy received the second e-mail, he looked through his binoculars and checked for unusual boat traffic. When all was clear, he loaded up the Zodiac and proceeded with care.

Itchy had made this trip before, but it was in the early days of preparation and he was a bit unfamiliar with the ever-changing landscape. He pulled into the cove without incident but had trouble locating the hinged tunnel door cover.

While dragging large branches to cover his small craft, he fortuitously spotted the rusty door. He attached the four briefcases to a large pole, swung the pole over his shoulder like a baseball bat, and carried them into the tunnel system that led to all the silos—including Freddie's.

* * *

Mundo was furious. "Who tha hell were dem otha guys out there on tha island?"

"What other guys? What are you talking about?" Maria cried.

"There were two guys out there at tha same place as yo' told us tha treasure was hidden, 'n' they were armed. Who the fuck were they, 'n' where the fuck did they hide da treasure?" he screamed before slapping her face.

Maria was shaking with fear as Mundo's henchmen sealed her mouth with duct tape and restrained her.

Mundo slowly lit a large cigar. After taking a few puffs, he said, "I don't want ta hurt yo', baby, so talk!"

A wide-eyed Maria wet herself and tried to scream through the tape. Mundo pulled a small part of the tape away from her mouth and asked, "Where be da loot?"

Maria shook her head furiously from side to side, and her eyes widened even more as Mundo placed the hot end of the cigar to her exposed leg. She writhed and bucked like a wild bronco as Mundo burned her exposed arms and legs.

When she collapsed in pain and exhaustion, Mundo asked again, "Where be da booty?"

Mundo did learn that Manny's partner was Andy Hastings and that he knew about the treasure and maybe double-crossed Manny and sent those men. Maria gave up Andy's address and continued to deny knowing anything else.

This time, Mundo pulled out an evil-looking knife and waved the blade in front of her face. Maria just hung her head and waited for the inevitable.

Mundo and his crew drove to Andy's house and found Andy's wife sitting at the kitchen table handicapping horses from the daily paper.

"And what the fuck do you ugly niggers want?" She glared at them.

* * *

Andy and Manny met at Hurley's bar and took a table in the rear. They ordered a pitcher of beer and a pair of cheeseburgers with fries.

"First off, I want to apologize to you, Manny. I was stuck with the cops and didn't know if they were interviewing you all night, so I called Lynch Turner. I was frantic, scared, and greedy. I would have split the loot with you, but I needed to secure it first."

"I also want to apologize. I thought the cops might break you, so I acted fast. I know Maria still keeps in contact with the Outlaws, so I called her. I now know I acted hastily for the same reasons as you. I'm sorry."

"You didn't have her use that big black gangster, Mundo, did you?" Andy laughed.

"Yes, I did." Manny laughed back.

Andy and Manny shook hands, and all was forgiven. They knew they had a tough task on their hands. They had to search the island during daylight, and it had to be during the brief period when the burials were suspended.

The two guards also had to contend with the Black Outlaws gang, which also knew about the treasure. They kicked around some ideas while enjoying the beer and burgers. Finally, they decided to fix it so the Outlaws took the fall for killing the Irish Patriots. They couldn't set the police on them. Otherwise, the treasure would no longer be a secret. The two decided to let the Irish Patriots do their dirty work for them. Lynch Turner, unfortunately, would become collateral damage.

"Manny, I found out that the investigators are through on Hart Island, so let's head out there ourselves and conduct a search. We can rent a small motorboat from Rosenberg's and pretend to go fishing. I'll also get word out to the Irish that the Outlaws killed J. K. and Waldo. You have Maria get word to the Outlaws that the island is still too hot to visit. This should give us time to find the treasure while the Outlaws stay away. I don't think the Irish know why the Outlaws offed their pals, but they will exact revenge nonetheless. It's a win-win situation for us." Andy grinned.

* * *

As Andy and Manny were meeting in Hurley's bar, a dark-gray Mercedes SUV drove up to the Black Outlaws clubhouse on Creston Avenue in the South Bronx.

Mundo was playing pool, as usual, when the Molotov cocktail came crashing through the rear window. The drapes and wall burst into flames.

The clubhouse was a tinder box of dried wood and plasterboard that would erupt into an inferno. Eight Outlaws knew it would be insane to attempt to put out the flames by blocking the back door, so the terrified gangsters ran for the front.

Mundo exited first. As he took in a long breath of fresh air, his lungs were immediately filled with lead. Shot five times in the chest, he fell in a heap in the doorway.

The remaining Outlaws froze. Bubba ran to the rear of the clubhouse and barged through the back door to escape.

Bubba emerged covered in flames. He rolled on the ground and flailed about helplessly as the fire engulfed his body.

As air rushed in through the two opened doors, the fire flashed into an all-out conflagration. The other hoods were running in circles as the ceiling crashed down on top of them. Two men ran for the front door and were immediately cut down in a hail of bullets. The others died painful deaths as their cries for help were ignored.

The gray Mercedes drove off.

* * *

It was a beautiful summer day, so Micko and Esmeralda walked the four blocks to the City Island Diner. It was a quaint little place that had a flexible menu along with dozens of home-baked goods.

"Let's sit back there." Esmeralda pointed to a cozy corner booth.

When they were seated, a middle-aged woman with a weather-beaten face barked, "What will ya have?"

"Hello, Maggie. I'll just have my regular cappuccino," Esmeralda said.

"Oh hi, Emmy, I didn't recognize you with that damn sun piercing the window right into my eyes." She laughed. "And what will your fella have?"

Maggie gave Micko the once-over and smiled her approval to Esmeralda.

"I'll have a coffee, milk and two sugars," Micko said.

"I'll bring you the coffee plain, and you can do whatever you damn well please to it," she growled as she left for the coffee counter.

"Maggie takes a little while to get used to," Esmeralda said with a smile.

"She seems to take to you...*Emmy*."

"Yeah, she's cool. Emmy is my nickname."

When Maggie returned with the coffee, she flashed a pleasant smile and left without a word.

After each took a sip of java, Micko asked, "So what do you know about Hart Island?"

Esmeralda took a deep breath before she explained the island's history that went back to the Civil War. In 1864, colored soldiers were trained there, then Confederate prisoners were imprisoned there until the end of the war. During the 1870 yellow fever epidemic, people were quarantined on Hart Island. After that, a women's psychiatric center was erected, then a sanatorium for those suffering from tuberculosis. Later, it was a prison and workhouse for delinquent boys.

Micko was amazed at how she ran down the history without pausing for thoughts. Her jade eyes glowed as she spoke.

He already knew that the island had become a potter's field many years ago and that the Department of Transportation provided ferryboat service for the Department of Corrections.

Esmeralda continued her dissertation, saying a drug rehabilitation center called Phoenix House was located there until 1976 and explaining that many historic buildings were still intact but in disrepair.

Micko reached out and touched her hand. "Emmy, you are amazing."

"Oh, I forgot to tell you the best part." She was almost giddy. "During the Cold War, Hart Island was home to a dozen Nike Ajax missiles."

"You gotta be kidding me!"

The couple barely touched their coffee as they discussed the storied history of Hart Island. Micko asked, "How do you know so much about this?"

"Well, it's a long story," she said.

"Maggie, two more of the same over here," Micko begged with a smile.

Esmeralda told about growing up in Spain as an only child and how her parents were strict. She lived an opulent lifestyle and went to the finest boarding schools money could buy. Her father was an art professor who taught at various universities until his appointment at the Prado Museum in Madrid.

Religion and a strict code of morality played a big part in her upbringing. Boys and dating were out of the question. Her parents were angered that she couldn't find a subject to excel in. She didn't care for the arts. She cared about gaining as much knowledge about as many things as possible.

Esmeralda was a bit shy while divulging her past to Micko, but she continued.

Micko learned that Esmeralda and her mother came to the United States six years earlier after her father died. Spain's archaic pension and laws regarding family wills basically left Esmeralda and her mother penniless. They came to City Island to live with her uncle Reuben.

Esmeralda stopped for a moment to sip her cappuccino. She looked Micko in the eye, smiled, and continued. A year after moving in with Reuben, he took ill and died of lung cancer. He had willed the small cottage to her and her mother. Esmeralda gave piano lessons while her mother toiled in a sail-stitching shop on City Island.

Esmeralda laughed as she recounted how poor they suddenly became. Her mother continued the strict upbringing, even though Esmeralda was far into womanhood. She told Micko that she never socialized and on rare occasions dated Mexican laborers who worked in the numerous restaurants in this seaside community. These poorly educated men offered her little in cerebral interaction, and she never dated anyone a second time.

She stopped and looked at Micko with green, puppy-dog eyes. "I hope you don't think I'm a prude or antisocial with men. It's just that I didn't meet any under my mother's watchful eyes, and the ones who hit on me were intellectually dull."

Micko laughed and gently touched her hand again. "Believe me, I understand. These days most people are too busy with work and career goals to have time to find a qualified date. I guess the intellectual part and pork-chop hair leave me out."

They both laughed heartily until Micko moved his hands, signaling her to continue.

After her mother died, Esmeralda took a job in the public library on City Island. She had a voracious appetite for reading and gaining knowledge about her surroundings. Librarian fit the bill. She could read all she wished and almost all the time. She had access to local ancient manuscripts found nowhere else in the world. The history of City Island and the surrounding area fascinated her, plus she was now in a government job with all of its benefits.

"Does that answer your question, Detective?" she asked with a smile.

"You were right. That was a long story," he deadpanned.

Esmeralda laughed as she childishly slapped his arm.

"Oh, I almost forgot." Micko fumbled through his briefcase and removed the two coins.

Esmeralda's eyes blazed. "Where did you get these?"

"These are the coins I was telling you about. This is why I believe there is treasure that leads to murder."

"Well, we'd better get back to the library and research these coins, me swabbie," she teased.

Micko thought, *I like this green-eyed devil.*

* * *

Lynch was assigned to guard prisoners in the notorious F block. These were savage prisoners who were waiting to be transferred to prison to serve their long sentences. Convicted of heinous crimes that would send them to upstate prisons for long stretches, they were kept temporarily in this special cellblock.

He never befriended any of these cons, since they would be moved once they received their sentences. Hard-boiled convicts, but short-timers in F block.

Lynch felt a need to relieve himself, so he told another guard, "I have to drain the lizard. I'll be back in a minute."

He walked lazily to the officers' restroom and did his business. Lynch never saw or heard the tall man lurking in the shadows. He felt someone lift his shirt, and then he fell to the floor squirming uncontrollably. He had just been hit with seven hundred thousand volts from a stun gun.

Lynch was helpless as he was dragged from the urinal into a cramped toilet stall. He felt his trouser belt being removed and tied tightly around his neck.

"Where is it?" a deep voice growled.

Lynch knew he was in no position to argue or negotiate, so he sputtered, "It's still hidden on Hart Island. Nobody knows where except the dead Irish. I swear to you. I swear!"

The belt tightened, and Lynch floated off into permanent unconsciousness. The tall man tied the loose end of the belt to the highest point on the flusher and left. He had business to attend to at Hart Island.

* * *

Freddie was pacing around in his underground office when Itchy arrived with the bags.

"What's up, boss?" Itchy asked.

Freddie explained the raid on his drug business to his trusted pal.

"Gee, boss, what're you going to do for dough?"

"There is a silver lining to this mess. I've completed a double batch of high-grade heroin for our offshore friends. I'll just move up the delivery date, and that will give me enough pocket money for now."

"I don't know. Those guys aren't going to like that. Those Dominicans don't like any change of plans. They're too cautious."

"Fuck them and their caution. I need money, and I need it now! I can't get at my savings accounts. I'm virtually homeless except for this fortress."

He quickly sent a text to the Dominican buyers:

Freddie: Must move reunion up a week. Sickness in the family. Must travel.

Manuel: Don't like to reschedule.

Freddie: It will be twice as much fun. Same time same place when I can see your sunny face @ noon.

Freddie studied his pal for a moment, trying to decide if he should tell him about the gold and silver pieces. He knew Itchy was a functioning heroin addict but had been reliable and loyal.

"Come here. I want to show you something," Freddie said as he put his hand on Itchy's shoulder."

Freddie led Itchy through a series of underground passageways with the aid of a flashlight. Itchy was unfamiliar with this area, which was ill lit and smelled of some kind of obnoxious fuel.

Freddie opened a heavy metal door that led into a cavernous room. Itchy saw the shadowy outlines of tall, colorful, metal cylinders lined up against the far wall.

"Boss, it stinks in here."

"Yes, yes it does," Freddie said.

In one corner of the room sat a large wooden table with a stack of rolled-up schematics and diagrams. Freddie lit a couple of candles to give Itchy the full effect of the view.

The south wall had dozens of missile cones and fins lined up neatly with other large pieces of military hardware. The north wall was lined with Geiger counters and full hazardous-material suits, along with an elevator.

"Does that thing work?" Itchy pointed to the elevator.

"It sure does. All I had to do was change the fuses and give it some oil." Freddie beamed. "It goes up to the surface near the missile silo next to the baby cemetery. When I throw this switch, the silo hatch will open. This switch sets the elevator in motion."

Freddie explained that this was how the army moved heavy missile objects up and down.

"What are those smelly cylinders for?" Itchy asked.

"I'm not sure, but they're probably filled with rocket fuel."

"Holy shit! Isn't that stuff dangerous?"

"Probably, but there are lots of rooms down here that are filled with these canisters. Just don't fuck with them." Freddie laughed.

"Now take a look at this," Freddie walked to a desk and chair next to the cylinders and pulled a metal dolly from behind the fuel containers. Sitting on the pallet was an opened chest of gold and silver coins.

Itchy's eyes almost popped out of his head. "Boss, you're rich. Who needs heroin? You have millions."

"You, my friend, need heroin, and I need a safe way to sell this treasure."

The two spent hours separating older coins dated from the fifteenth century to the coins stamped 1645 or later. Freddie's research taught him that the Spanish coined the earlier money with purer gold and silver. Later coins were less pure and minted by local merchants. Ironic how the gold and heroin were processed similarly.

The two filled one orange Pelican case with the richer coins and mixed the yellow case with scraps of iron and metal that littered the floor. The rest of the coins were returned to the chest and placed back behind the lethal fuel.

Itchy took note that what he thought was water pooling on the floor was actually seepage from the cylinders causing the stench.

As Freddie led Itchy back to his office, Itchy carefully memorized the route.

Freddie opened the two other bags that Itchy had brought, and a sly smile appeared on his face. "You did well, my friend."

The first duffel bag was lined with several automatic assault rifles and extra clips of ammo. The second case was filled with hand grenades and handguns.

Expecting a bloody drug war against his enemies, Freddie traded heroin to the Albanian mob for weapons. The Albanians imported the weapons from Kosovo, whose dealers traded with the Russians. The weapons came into Newark hidden in shipping containers with auto parts. They were then trucked in plain sight to a mansion in the sleepy town of Leonia, New Jersey. Within a magnificent view of the Hudson River and the Palisades, the gangsters stored all kinds of illegal goods.

The duo spent the rest of the day booby-trapping their sanctuary as Freddie kept a detailed map of each placement.

After a delicious surf-and-turf meal, Freddie directed Itchy to take the Zodiac back to the *Who Nose* and move the boat closer to a cove at David's Island. They also made a crude sign that they hoped would fool the cops. The *Who Nose* became *On the Run*.

∗   ∗   ∗

"Paco, Freddie wants to move up the next buy," Manuel said.

"Details," Paco said.

"He wants to meet us at the same place at noon tomorrow. He has a double batch to sell. It seems he must flee his den for a while. He might be too hot at this time."

"That's all right. I think we should relieve him of his product and end our relationship, cost free."

∗   ∗   ∗

Micko and Esmeralda returned to the library and sat at a table with comfortable leather-padded chairs. She hoisted a stack of ancient books onto the table, and they began investigating the mysterious coins.

They learned that the gold coin was known as a gold escudo, first minted in Spain in 1535. The silver and gold escudos were the common currency for most of the trading world until the mid-nineteenth century, when the United States began a competitive minting process.

The escudo was minted in a variety of denominations: one-half, one, two, four, and eight. They were known as reals. The gold eight-escudo coin was known as a doubloon. The gold was heated until it could be hammered into a coin shape, and then a hand-pressed seal was stamped into the soft metal. The seal designated the current king of Spain, and the year was imprinted. A letter *M* indicated that the coin was minted in Madrid. An *S* indicated that it was minted in Seville.

Esmeralda located a microscope, and the two sleuths were able to read the date as 1607. The Spanish seal corresponded to the seal of King Carlos II. The microscope also helped them make out the letter *S* and the number 8.

"What you have there, Detective, is a rare Spanish doubloon," Esmeralda said with a wink.

"Let's check out the silver one," he said excitedly.

Using the same methods through the National Numismatic Collection of the Smithsonian Institution's National Museum of American History, they learned about the silver escudo.

Like the gold doubloon, the silver coin, called a real, was hammered into shape by hand and stamped. The silver coin was made in several sizes, but an eight-reale was often cut up like a pizza into eight pieces. Each piece had its own denomination—thus the term "pieces of eight."

"Well, Emmy, it looks like my piece of eight is an eight real," Micko said with a smile.

The silver was too smooth and worn to read a country seal, but it did appear that the two coins came from pirate booty on Hart Island.

Micko's cell phone rang, and he could see that it was Chief Clifford.

"Yes, Chief," he answered.

"Where are my reports?"

Micko gave him a quick update and apologized for the delay in the reports.

"Listen to me, O'Shaughnessy. Whatever you do, don't speak to that inspector general from Corrections," the chief warned.

"Who, Tom Sullivan?"

"Yes. That prick closed out the drowning case as an unfortunate accident, and he has all the investigative DD5s from Detective McCarthy, but he is snooping around asking questions about your parallel investigation."

"Why would the IG do that?" Micko asked.

"I don't know. I think he's afraid we will turn up something that will make him look bad."

"Something to make him look bad…there are now eight dead bodies associated with this case."

"No, make that nine. Rikers guard Lynch was found in the officer's bathroom with a belt tied around his neck. It appears to be a self-inflicted hanging, but I sent your partner, Gus Lopez, to the county morgue to ask questions from the coroner. The medical examiner located two small burn marks on Lynch's body that could have come from a powerful stun gun. The hanging appears to have been staged."

Micko took a moment to digest this information and said, "Chief, this is spiraling out of control."

"You stay on this case, Micko. I trust you to solve this mess."

Micko explained the developments to Esmeralda. The entire murder and treasure mystery excited the hell out of her. Her emerald-green eyes widened and radiated when he told her about Lynch's staged suicide.

"How about dinner? I'm starved," Micko said.

"Sure. How about taking me to the Morris Yacht Club?"

"With all these fancy restaurants on City Island, why the Morris?"

"I'm not into fancy. I'm into history and charming. I've read that the Morris Yacht Club is both."

"Yes, it is. I like it very much. It's also casual dress for dinner, so we can be comfortable. I'll drive you home to get changed, and I'll go to my kayak club and freshen up."

They exchanged phone numbers, and Micko walked her to his car.

"Aren't you a little old for this machine?" she teased.

"I am not," he teased back.

Micko looked admiringly at Esmeralda as he drove the short distance to her house. It was a quaint wood-framed cottage, freshly painted white with green trim. It sat on a dead-end street accompanied by three similar homes. Huge elm trees gave the street a sense of solitude and secrecy.

"I'll call you when I'm ready." Esmeralda gave Micko a warm smile as she exited the Firebird and walked up the four stone stairs leading to the front door.

* * *

Micko drove to the kayak club, washed up, and grabbed a beer from the fridge. Just as he was about to take the first sip, his cell phone rang. A quick glance showed it was Chief Clifford.

The conversation was intense as Micko worked his brain, trying to comprehend. He was ordered to bring this case to a close before the news media put it all together.

No sooner had he ended his conversation when the phone rang again.

"No more bad news, Chief. I'm still digesting what you just told me."

"I'll be your chief if you will be my little Indian," Esmeralda cooed.

"Oh, sorry, I thought you were—"

"I know." She laughed. "I don't know what I'm looking forward to more: your last conversation with the other chief or my dinner."

It took Micko ten minutes to drive from the kayak club to Esmeralda's house. When he pulled in front of the house, she made a grand exit from her humble doorway.

Micko was mesmerized by the metamorphosis from dull caterpillar to extraordinary butterfly. Esmeralda was absolutely stunning. She wore an almost sheer, lime-colored, spaghetti-strap summer dress that stopped at her knees.

Her hair, which had been wrestled into a tight bun, was now flowing over her dainty shoulders. In the setting sun, her hair was ablaze in a mass of auburn with carefully added blond streaks. Gone were the unfashionable eyeglasses and dowdy clothing.

"You look spectacular," Micko said with a stutter.

"Yes, I do," she mocked with a smile.

Micko opened the car door for her and got a pleasant whiff of her perfume.

"I don't know if I'll be able to keep my eyes on the road. Your looks are absolutely tantalizing."

"You'd better keep your eyes on the road, buster. I'm longing for a ride to the restaurant, not the hospital." She laughed.

During the short ride to the club, Micko gave Esmeralda its brief description and history.

The Morris Yacht Club is over 150 years old. It was originally a three-story white wooden Victorian mansion that traded hands with wealthy men until it became a hotel and fell into the possession of Columbia University.

In 1937, it became the yacht club and a regular hangout for City Island residents and tourists alike. The club members worked tirelessly to maintain the building and marina.

In 2006, a freak fire devastated the main building, and it had to be rebuilt from scratch. With its million-dollar views of the Long Island Sound and Eastchester Bay, there was little doubt among City Island residents that the club would rise like a phoenix from the ashes.

Esmeralda clapped her hands childishly. "Thank you, Professor Marvel, for that eloquent discourse."

"Are you mocking me?" he asked teasingly.

She flashed a smile and showed him her glorious green eyes. She was pleased he had discarded the filthy tie and suit coat. With his business-style shirt opened at the collar and hair neatly combed, he looked ruggedly handsome.

Micko parked in the massive lot next to the club's restaurant, and the two walked like they were on their way into their prom. The hostess seated them on the top floor's wraparound deck with an exclusive view of the New York City skyline.

"This is gorgeous, and what a magnificent view." Esmeralda was genuinely impressed.

"I love this particular table, since I can see right between the huge weeping willows and have an unencumbered view of the city's skyline," Micko said.

The restaurant was oddly unoccupied and offered the couple nice privacy. After ordering drinks, Esmeralda said, "So tell me what the chief told you."

She had a look of anticipation that a child has on Christmas morning.

"The chief has assigned all nine homicides to me, and me alone. The Corrections IG wants to take complete control of the case, and I'm being ordered to solve this nightmare before politics rears its ugly head and makes us all look bad."

"But how can you work any faster? You are doing everything you can."

"Well, I'm not going to worry about it tonight," he said with a smile.

The couple had a pleasant dinner filled with stimulating conversation about the complex case and traded ideas.

The two sat silently sipping their after-dinner drink as the sun set in an orange blaze.

The dinner check was paid, and Micko looked deep into Esmeralda's eyes. He felt awkward and clumsily held her hand as they walked back to his car.

Micko opened the door for Esmeralda, and she leaned up and planted a soft, wet kiss on his lips.

"Does that help?" she asked tenderly.

"It does."

That cue removed his tension, and they laughed all the way back to her house.

Micko parked in front of her small cottage and opened the car door for her. Esmeralda smiled at him and withdrew a set of house keys from her dainty lime-green purse.

The front door led to a small vestibule craftily decorated with a nautical theme. As they entered the interior, Micko saw that the furnishings were aged.

Brass Stiffel lamps sat on small doily-covered tables. Ancient portraits adorned the walls, and historic memorabilia sat on the fireplace mantel. A brown three-seat couch covered with an ivory throw sat next to an orange wing-backed chair. The living room was exceptionally clean but decorated like that of an older woman.

Esmeralda watched Micko take in the surroundings.

"Kind of overused, don't you think?" she asked.

"You don't look overused to me," Micko said.

"Quite the contrary, I assure you." She laughed. "I mean the furnishings. They belonged to my uncle, and he never evolved with the times. He kept the place the way my aunt furnished it nearly fifty years ago.

"When Uncle died, my mother kept things the same. When my lawyers finally settle my mother's estate, I will refurnish this place with contemporary furniture and art."

Micko was observing a set of desktop photos when she sneaked up behind him and whispered, "My mother was old-fashioned, but I am not."

With that, she turned him around and threw her slender arms around his neck. Esmeralda looked into Micko's hazel eyes and without another word planted a wet kiss on his lips.

She flickered her tongue, amateurishly, around the inside of Micko's mouth like a flag dancing in the wind. It was painfully obvious that she lacked experience in the art of making out.

Micko gently pulled back, held her head in his hands, and gave her a warm, sweet, slow kiss on her full lips. Then he parted her lips with his tongue and smoothly pirouetted his tongue with hers.

Esmeralda let out a sigh of satisfaction as the two kissed for what seemed like an eternity. Micko held her closer and tighter as the kissing became more heated and sensual.

Esmeralda gently pulled back and let Micko watch as she flicked the thin straps off her shoulders and let her dress slide to the floor.

Her eyes were ablaze, and her chest heaved with every breath.

Micko looked at her incredible figure. He knew that she was braless when he felt her erect nipples pressing against his chest as they kissed. Now he could see that she also went commando. Her pubic hair was closely cropped.

Esmeralda was giving him that *take me now* look as he picked her up and carried her into the first bedroom he encountered. He gently placed her on the bed and quickly undressed as she watched his every move.

She sighed at the sight of his arousal and reached for him.

Micko lay next to Esmeralda, passionately kissed her lips and neck, and moved to her sensitive ears. She moaned with delight as his tongue explored her erogenous zones.

He slowly stimulated each sensitive part of her body. Micko paid special attention to her full, shapely breasts. As he kissed and licked her body, his hands and neatly groomed nails expertly foraged across her skin. She was highly aroused.

He got a strong reaction to kissing and caressing her belly button as he headed south. Before he even touched her vaginal area, she gasped, "Oh my God, oh my God!"

Micko parted her labia with his fingers and artfully tongued his way through her moist vagina. He licked and sucked and read her reactions to each sensitive area. Finally, he worked the clitoris, and Esmeralda nearly fell off the bed. She reacted like she had just been struck by lightning, with arms and legs flailing and her back arching.

"Oh God, oh God," she repeated over and over.

The experienced detective softly stuck his middle finger into her vagina and caressed her G-spot while his thumb swirled around her clit. He moved his mouth back to hers and kissed her passionately while his hand worked its magic.

Micko paid close attention to her every move and reaction to his touch and knew what tempo would bring her to climax. He teased her a bit.

"Oh God, oh God," she repeated as she arched her back and came to an explosive orgasm.

Esmeralda panted as if she had just run a marathon. Her sweet body glistened as she hugged Micko as tightly as she could. He returned her affection by gently kissing her face.

She let go to lie back on the bed, seemingly exhausted. Micko knew he had done well as he walked into the bathroom and wet a facecloth with warm water and grabbed a towel.

Micko washed her vaginal area with the wet cloth and patted her perspiring body with the towel. He placed the linen on a nightstand and caressed her hair.

"I never expected that," she said, still gasping.

"That's just foreplay." Micko laughed.

"My sex life has been a couple of unfulfilled, two-minute encounters with sexually selfish men. I've never encountered foreplay or an orgasm that I didn't give myself." She laughed too.

"Do you mind if I explore your body?" she asked.

"I encourage you to do so."

"Because of my lack of experience, I've read many books on erotica. I've just never had a chance to act out any of the fantasies they produced."

Esmeralda looked deeply into Micko's eyes as she ran her hands across his body. She started with his chest and arms and sensuously worked her way to his groin. She watched as his breathing changed when she touched his manhood.

Micko was highly excited as Esmeralda slid down the bed and played with his family jewels. She carefully studied his apparatus as if she were seeing one for the first time. She lifted it and pulled it and bent it with aroused curiosity.

"Study it, but please don't break it," Micko said.

She looked up at him with a devilish smile. Esmeralda had never had the opportunity to satisfy her curiosities about the male anatomy. She was genuinely enjoying her examination.

Finally, she softly touched the velvet penis head and watched her student's response. She combined a variety of touches, strokes, and licks until she knew what areas caused the greatest response from her man.

She learned quickly how to stimulate her detective. She slowly licked and sucked her way around Micko's penis and ball sack until he was writhing with pleasure.

He teased me; now it's my turn, she thought.

Esmeralda watched his reaction to her touches and rhythm and knew she was bringing him to the brink of orgasm. Every time he came close, she slowed her tempo or took her mouth away.

Suddenly, she stopped and climbed onto his rigid shaft. Her hair was dangling wildly. Her breasts swayed above his face as she moaned with delight. Her eyes rolled back as she mounted him and rocked in a sexual salsa.

Micko was about to explode as he watched Esmeralda spread her lips in a sensual grin. Constantly correcting her hip position to get maximum effect from her gyrations, she rode on him until her vaginal juices soaked his groin.

They exploded with intensity and moaned simultaneously.

Esmeralda's body shivered while she remained in her position. Eventually, she lay down with her breasts against Micko's.

"That was unbelievable. I freaking *love* sex!" she cried with a laugh.

"Is it all you thought it would be?" he asked.

"Better, much goddamn better. Erotic books are great, but one has to really have the sexual experience to enjoy sex."

"That sounds a bit analytical," he mused.

"My entire life has been analytical, without experiencing anything. I'm a prolific reader, but I'm going to have to have more practical experience in life."

The sex-exhausted couple lay in each other's arms talking and joking until sleep engulfed them.

Chapter 13

Andy and Manny met at Rosenberg's boat rentals on City Island. They parked in the customer lot and gathered their gear, fishing poles, and a large gunny sack with digging tools and flashlights.

The skiff with outboard engine was inexpensive and easily rode them to Hart Island. Andy had rechecked, and the IG's investigation was over. The island should be desolate.

They beached the small craft at the point where they could easily walk to the Phoenix House building. Each guard was secretly hiding his excitement. Andy would get rich, retire, and leave his squandering wife. Manny daydreamed about the riches he would bestow on his magnificent Maria.

They left the useless fishing gear aboard the skiff and carried the digging tools. The two were completely unaware of the disaster that had occurred in the fine, lush grass as they trampled through it on their way to the roadway.

When they reached the entrance to the Phoenix House, Manny excitedly declared, "We're here!"

Andy walked in first and nervously looked at the mud pile. It was obvious that a large portion of the mud had been removed and the chest with it. Manny looked around the huge room and found no evidence of mud tracks away from the pile.

"Earlier Mundo told Maria that the Irish were gunned down while walking away from here, and they didn't have the treasure with them. Where the hell did they move it to?" Manny asked.

Andy bent down near the mud pile and studied it carefully.

"Manny, I think it was removed by the backhoe. Look how clean the mud-hole is. If shovels had dug here, it would be a complete mess. It looks like the hole was made by one large scoop, and only the backhoe's front loader could do that."

Manny took a curious look. "I think you're right, but where did they take it?"

Before Andy could respond, a tall man slid out from the shadows of a crumpling stairway and fired two rapid shots into his back. Instead of running, a startled Manny turned to face the attacker. Just as his face registered both recognition and shock, he was felled by two bullets to the chest.

Tall Man learned all he needed to know. Unknown parties had moved the treasure to an unknown location on this godforsaken island. He bent down to check his handiwork and rose when he was sure the two were dead.

A supermarket shopping cart was lying inside this crumbling structure, and he used it to transport the bodies to the beach. Tall Man dragged the bodies by their collars through the sand and into their rented boat.

Tall Man had been moored in a blue-and-white sailboat offshore watching the comings and goings of the island. He saw a cabin cruiser named *Who Nose* drop anchor and a fellow drive a Zodiac to a hidden knoll at the north end of Hart Island. Hours later, he saw the man exit the cave-like area and take the Zodiac back to the *Who Nose* cabin cruiser.

He watched in curiosity as the motorboat was moved close to shore at David's Island a mere half-mile away. The Zodiac and pilot then returned to the cave.

Now Tall Man drove the bodies of Andy and Manny in their rented skiff to David's Island, where the cabin cruiser was anchored. He stepped up on the outer swim platform and quickly removed the crappy poster with the boat name *On the Run*. He had seen the Zodiac man clumsily hammer it over the original name, *Who Nose*.

Tall Man reached down, grabbed each man, and lifted both from the skiff to the swim platform and then onto the boat deck. Then he dragged them, one at a time, across the shiny deck and down into the galley and sleeping quarters.

Each body was placed into the storage locker under a sleeping bunk. The boat slept four, and now two rested in eternal slumber under two beds.

Tall Man rode the skiff back to Hart Island, where he had hidden his small rowboat. He attached the dinghy to the Rosenberg motorboat and towed it back to his rented sailboat. This was much easier than rowing the dinghy.

He returned to spying on Hart Island. Tall Man was prepared for the long haul. He had stocked up on wine, cheese, and a large variety of other comforts.

Tall Man had grown up in Long Island and learned how to sail as a child, so he was proficient in the art. He was pleased with the way things were progressing.

Chapter 14

Esmeralda served Micko a cup of coffee in bed and climbed back in with java in hand. The two were still naked from their carnal pleasures the night before.

Secure in their nakedness, the two jabbed each other about their date and romantic interlude.

Micko confided that he was delighted to have a bright, sexy, thirtyish, virginal lover. Esmeralda said she was equally delighted to have an older, experienced lover.

"Hmm...I called you bright and sexy. You referred to me as older. That's it? Older?"

"Well, you're not that bad looking for being older."

The banter continued while they sipped their coffee. They took a shower together before going back to the library for more research.

It was early, and the library was empty. Micko and Esmeralda picked a rear table complete with computers. They had agreed that Esmeralda would research local pirates and try to ascertain which one might have buried treasure on Hart Island. Micko would research the silos on Hart Island and try to locate schematics detailing the catacombs that crisscrossed the island.

They silently researched for hours. As the librarian, Esmeralda occasionally had to help out visitors. At other times, the researchers would rummage through old manuscripts that this local library was famous for.

The plan was to work until lunch and share what each had learned. Lunch would convene at the City Island Diner.

"Wadda ya got, me swabbie?" she asked.

"Hunger pains. What do you have?"

"Let's go to lunch and compare investigations."

They held hands as they walked to the diner and seated themselves at a quiet rear table.

"Why do you have to sit so far away? Just to make me walk farther," said a hostile Maggie.

Micko ignored her and ordered a corned beef on rye with plenty of mustard.

"I feel like a pint 'o spiced rum," Esmeralda quipped with a laugh.

"Not unless you have an eye patch and a parrot on your shoulder," Maggie said.

"OK, OK, I'll have my usual cappuccino and a Caesar salad."

Maggie shot Micko a surly look and dashed off with their lunch orders.

"Ladies first. Emmy, what did you find out about the local pirates?" Micko asked.

"Well, there were many more than I had anticipated. Did you know that Long Island was a safe haven for pirates and that they came from all over the world?"

"I did not know that."

"Besides harboring pirates, they built large compounds where they lived and raised little pirates."

"Were they born with wooden legs and eye patches and given parrots on their birthday?" Micko asked with a sly smile.

Esmeralda ignored him. "The best case for a pirate burying his loot on Hart Island is Captain Kidd."

"Are you *Kidd*-ing me?"

"This is serious. Captain Kidd was born in Scotland but immigrated to New York City. It was called New Amsterdam then. He married a wealthy widow named Sarah and had a daughter, also named Sarah. They lived in a waterfront mansion next to the harbor."

"It sounds like Kidd did very well for himself," Micko said.

"That he did, but he was a sorry-assed pirate. He had a good reputation as a seafarer and captained many ships, mostly as a privateer."

"What's a privateer?"

"A privateer was a private person or ship that engaged in maritime warfare under a commission of war. Kidd was a privateer for England during its war against France."

"Then why do you call him a poor excuse of a pirate?"

"This is kind of comical. He was given a huge thirty-four cannon warship and hired by the king of England and several New Amsterdam investors to hunt down French and pirate ships. He was to plunder the ships and split the cargo with the king and various investors. One of the investors was Lord Bellomont, the governor of New Amsterdam."

"So what's so funny about that?"

"Well, when he sailed his new warship, the *Adventure Galley*, into New York Harbor, Kidd paraded about like a gay peacock. He hired the finest seamen and soon had a crew of 150 top-notch sailors. When he departed New York Harbor, he passed an incoming British warship. Rumor has it that his sailors dropped their drawers and mooned the British Navy boys.

"The British ship retaliated by boarding Captain Peacock and relieving him of most of his best seamen. You see, the British ship was also coming to New York to recruit sailors.

"Now Captain Kidd had to sail back into New York with his tail between his legs and look for a new crew. The problem is that he was unreservedly mocked, and only low-life scurvy and ex-pirates were left to choose from."

Maggie brought the coffee as Esmeralda leaned forward with a look like the cat that ate the canary.

"You did damn good, Emmy, but why do you think he buried treasure so close to his home?"

"Well, his privateering orders gave him papers to take *only* French and pirate vessels. He was commissioned to scour the Red Sea area, and after a year of searching, he had yet to capture a ship. His crew didn't care about Kidd's commission. They wanted booty from any ship at all. A particularly nasty gunner named William Moore wanted to attack an English merchant ship, and when Kidd declined, he tried to start a mutiny.

"Captain Kidd immediately killed the mutiny by killing Moore with an iron bucket to the head. Kidd felt this was justified on the high seas to terminate a mutiny."

"I'm still waiting for the treasure."

"Well, Kidd finally spotted a merchant ship flying French colors, and he attacked and scored a huge bounty. Unfortunately, most of the bounty belonged to the East India Company, which had close ties to Great Britain. Now politics played a big role in Kidd's fall from grace.

"Politics led to rumors of Captain Kidd turning from privateer to pirate, and British warships were sent out to arrest him. To make a long story short, Kidd was sure that his friend and investor, Lord Bellomont, would protect him, so he made a mad dash to meet with him in Boston.

"Captain Kidd knew how nefarious politics could be and feared Bellomont might betray him, so he hid treasure in several places while en route to New York and Boston.

"It is well documented that he hid some booty on Gardiners Island, and that bounty was dug up and recovered. The rest of his treasure went to the grave with him."

Micko looked at Esmeralda with pride. She had done a wonderful job with her research. "But what makes you think he buried some of the loot on Hart Island?"

"Well, looking at a variety of maps and shipping lanes used by vessels of the time, it's one of hundreds of islands that he could have hidden treasure on. He is the only well-known pirate who is known to have hidden treasure in this area," she said.

"I guess the odds are that you are right. To prove it, we will have to locate the treasure and find a provenance that it is indeed Kidd's. Whatever happened to the almost-pirate Kidd?"

"Well, he met the governor in Boston and was betrayed and jailed. Then he was sent to England, where he was hanged on the docks. Do you know that the first time they tried to hang him, the rope broke, and they had to hang him again? Some accounts have him breaking the rope twice and hanged on the third attempt. Anyway, his body was tarred, and he was left hanging in a metal cage as a warning to all sailors who might consider life as a pirate. The funny thing is, he really wasn't a pirate at all."

"Very good, Nancy Drew," Micko said with a smile.

*　*　*

Police administrative aide Connie Walton walked into Sergeant Powers office.

"Sergeant, Hastings and Santiago are both AWOL, and there is no answer at their homes."

"Are they still being investigated by the IG?"

"No, sir, that investigation is over. They are supposed to be assigned to the hospital ward until next week, when they resume burial duties at Hart Island."

Sergeant Powers was easygoing, and he knew his administrative aide was at the top of her game.

"Connie, call roll call and see if there wasn't a mix-up and they weren't given double assignments."

"I already did that, sir. With that Turner incident, I think we should send a car to their homes."

Powers knew she was right. Both men were involved in the ferryboat incident, and they both knew Lynch Turner, who just committed suicide by hanging.

"All right, Connie, send a car to each home and have reports made."

*　*　*

"All right, Inspector Clouseau, what did *you* find out?" Emmy giggled.

"Besides the historic past, I concentrated on the massive underground passages. Ancient builders and soldiers were fond of creating escape tunnels between forts, homes, and special buildings.

"Each decade brought new buildings and new tunnels. Then when the army's Sixty-Sixth Antiaircraft Artillery Missile Battalion built Battery NY Fifteen, new tunnels were built."

"Why did the army build tunnels?" Emmy asked.

"It's kind of complicated. The army placed Nike Ajax missile silos on Hart Island and neighboring David's Island to thwart an attack by Soviet bombers. The integrated fire-control system that tracked the targets and directed missiles was located in Fort Slocum. Fort Slocum was located on David's Island."

"I get that, but why the tunnels?"

"The twenty-one-foot missiles were too big to stand in conventional silos, so they were placed in lengthwise silos, then raised by elevator-controlled launchers to a standing position when ready for liftoff. All the missiles had to be accessed and cared for from belowground since the aboveground silos were covered.

"This led to a complex set of underground tunnels, warehouses, turrets, tool and extra parts rooms, workers' lounges, cafeterias, huge fuel containers, and so on. There was more of a city underground than above."

"Why did the army abandon these silos?"

"From what I read, the army abandoned the site when the Soviet long-range bombers became obsolete."

"How the hell did long-range bombers become obsolete?"

"Intercontinental missiles replaced the bomber threat. The Ajax missile system was in effect from 1956 to 1961. In 1974, the army removed the last components of the missile system."

"I wonder how many people on City Island even know about those old missiles."

"I read that on Sunday mornings, the army engineers would sound an air-raid siren and raise a few of the rockets to test the system. Each week, a different set of missiles would be stood up and prepared for launch."

"That must have been very frightening for the residents, especially the children."

"I bet it was. In any event, the missiles are long gone, but the tunnels and hidden rooms must still be there. Knowing the army, I suspect they removed only the hardware and left the rest intact, including the huge generator."

"What generator?"

"Well, to raise those twenty-one-foot rockets on their launchers to a firing position required enormous power. I read that the generator was strong enough to power a city of ten thousand people. That's a lot of power."

Esmeralda was impressed with the depth of the detective's research, and she knew he was just dying to crawl into the labyrinth below Hart Island. Like a little kid, he would explore the ancient and decrepit hollows, no matter how dangerous it was.

*　*　*

Micko gave Esmeralda a tight hug and a gentle kiss on the lips as he said good-bye. He left her doing her job in the library while he raced back to his squad room to type up the reports he had been neglecting.

"Well, look who's back," Gus said as Micko walked through the door.

"Hi, partner. I hope your caseload hasn't increased that much," Micko said.

"Now why should my caseload increase? I'm catching your cases as well as my own, and this is July in the Bronx. Of course my caseload has increased, you Irish—"

Before he could finish, Micko said, "C'mon, Gus. I cover for you on occasion."

"What occasion? Oh yeah, you mean that time I was late coming home from Puerto Rico because of bad weather affecting my flight?"

"Yes, Gus, I had to pretend to be you when the patrol-duty captain arrived on the scene of *your* case. I signed you in as being present, and the case was assigned to you. I thought you would be your usual fifteen minutes late, not three hours."

"It was a funny case." Gus laughed.

"Yeah, the duty captain couldn't understand how a person could be hit by a train and look so normal. I explained that the train never touched him, but by being in the tunnel so close to the fast-moving train, the suction carried the body a hundred feet across the tracks, breaking every bone in his body but not causing much visual damage." Micko chuckled.

"His insides were like that of a scarecrow hanging in a cornfield, and the captain kept looking at the DOA, saying, 'How can this be?'"

"All right, Micko, you did a good job covering for me then, but I've had to cover for you during those escapades in the South Pacific."

"Yes, Gus, you're right. Let me type up some DD5s, and I'll buy you dinner."

"Now you're talking."

While Micko was making headway typing up his reports, he fielded a phone call from Chief Clifford.

"Micko, do you have any news for me? You are supposed to keep me informed."

"No, Chief, I'm just catching up on my reports, and then I'm going back to Hart Island to check out a few things that are bothering me."

"Well, you had better be careful. Andy and Manny are missing. They did not show up at work or call in to take the day off. Rikers security sent a car to their homes to check up on them and found both women murdered."

"What?" Micko screamed.

"Your ears aren't painted on. You heard me."

"Who killed the wives? Who is investigating?" he stammered.

"In addition, someone shot up the Black Outlaws clubhouse and killed Mundo and seven members of his gang. You're still the investigator on this, so you tell me. I'm sending you all the info in an attachment to your cell phone. You now have nineteen bodies. I want those DD5s pronto."

Micko was in shock. He sat looking at the telephone he had just hung up, barely believing what the chief had told him.

Gus knew the call was bad news. Nothing bothered Micko, but this case was unnerving him.

"What was that all about, buddy?"

"It seems my homicide rate on this case just rose to nineteen," Micko said.

Ten minutes later, Micko's cell phone pinged, and he saw the attachments from Chief Clifford. After reading the reports, Micko said, "C'mon, Gus. Let's go eat."

Gus drove to the Jolly Tinker, a family-oriented Irish bar that was known for its burgers. Micko approved of this choice and traded pleasantries with the bartender, Tom Martin.

A big-busted waitress named Sally seated them at a small table. They both ordered burgers and fries. When Sally delivered their food, Gus said softly, "I wonder how she can see the table place mats past that huge chest of hers."

"Practice, my boy, years of practice," she said.

"I guess she has big ears as well." Micko snickered.

After they finished their meals and polished off a pitcher of beer, Micko asked Sally for another. Then he looked at Gus and said, "I'm going to bring you up to date on my case."

"What's up, partner?"

"You are well aware of the two dirty corrections officers, Andy and Manny. Well, they have gone missing. When Rikers sent a car to their homes to find out why they were AWOL, they found Andy's wife, Peggy, tortured and murdered. Gutted like a fresh salmon."

"Holy shit!" Gus said.

"Manny's wife, Maria, was also tortured and skinned alive by someone who knew how to use a knife. I believe Maria's pals in the Outlaws tortured her thinking she knew where the treasure was moved to. Obviously, she didn't know but gave up Andy's house address, and they in turn tortured Peggy for the same information."

Micko took a long drink from his beer. "Gus, the Black Outlaws clubhouse was shot up and burned to the ground today, and eight members were killed. I believe the Irish Patriots are involved."

"This case is getting insane."

"The treasure is still on Hart Island, isn't it, Micko?"

"I think so, and I'm going to find it."

Chapter 15

Micko drove the short distance to his kayak club and quickly dressed in proper paddling gear. He wanted to do a quick survey of the burial area before dark.

Fifteen minutes later, he was pushing off during the end of the low tide. The paddling was easy, and he reached the island quickly because of a strong easterly wind.

Micko kayaked to the north end of the island, hooked right, and paddled toward the small beach. As he passed the northern point of the island, he was paddling close to shore to avoid the wind. Suddenly, he observed an unusual shape hidden among the brush.

He paddled closer and saw it was a Zodiac. He surmised it must have floated loose and washed up in this small cove. Upon closer examination, the detective realized that someone had attempted to hide the craft by covering it with loose branches.

Micko eased his kayak into the cove and pulled it onto the small sandy shelf next to the Zodiac. He stood over the Zodiac and studied it carefully.

Without warning, he felt like he was struck in the back and head simultaneously with a baseball bat. He lost consciousness and tumbled into the wayward boat.

Tall Man had not counted on this problem. He watched Hart Island for hours with no activity, so he decided to motor the Rosenberg rental boat to the beach area and watch this tiny cove.

His plan was to wait until Zodiac Man left the tunnel with the treasure. Tall Man was hoping that when Zodiac Man went to the *Who Nose*, he would relieve him, at gunpoint, of the booty.

He was just finishing covering the motorboat with loose brush when this kayaker appeared. *Oh well, just another bump in the road,* he thought.

Tall Man had to improvise with this unexpected annoyance, and he quickly devised a plan. He raced the rented motorboat, loaded with his kidnapped victim, through the stubborn waves until he reached his rented sailboat. He quickly tied the skiff to a rail and picked up the supplies necessary for his next task.

* * *

Tall Man had his prisoner hog-tied pretty well but could not move him in the daylight. July was a busy boater month, and the water traffic was hectic. He decided to leave the prisoner in the skiff while he relaxed and had a nice meal. Sunset would be here soon enough.

Tall Man was grilling fresh fish on the boat's deck when he heard his prisoner stirring, so with a glass of white wine in one hand and a stun gun in the other, he zapped the prisoner again.

When darkness came, the prisoner was still out cold and a bottle of wine was polished off. Tall Man climbed down into the skiff and raced off to complete his new task.

* * *

Freddie's situation grew from frustration to anger, then to fear and paranoia. He and Itchy completed their booby-trap brigade and had the traps mapped out so as not to kill themselves. He had escape routes planned and hiding spots with water and food if he had to hole up for any length of time. He even started snorting his own heroin, and this made him more paranoid.

Itchy still liked to sneak away and shoot up when things were quiet, but things were not quiet. He knew he couldn't get high and drift into that sweet dreamy bubble. He had to watch his lifelong pal, who was unraveling before his very eyes.

Freddie had placed weapons in hidden rooms and offices along the labyrinth. He was spaced out and convinced that either ghostly pirates or murderous cops were out to get him.

Itchy had trouble memorizing the locations of all the booby traps, and Freddie wouldn't part with the map. This caused a bit of trepidation. He knew the booby traps were set well and that if he forgot where one was placed, then death would be immediate.

Kaboom!

"What the fuck was that?" Freddie screamed.

* * *

Micko didn't know what woke him: the loud clanging of the warning buoy or the cool water sloshing up against his legs. His entire body was wracked with pain, as if he had been hit by a Mack truck.

It was dark, very dark. He was trying to gather his wits, but his head was foggy and his feet and hands were bound. *What's going on? Where am I?*

Moving about, he realized he was tethered, from the rear, to some fixed object in the water. He stayed still and waited until his eyes adjusted to the dark.

The water splashed up to his waistline, and he could make out the white crests of the waves. As his eyes adjusted, he saw that he was about a half-mile offshore from an island.

Micko looked about and realized he was tied to a rock formation. His head was throbbing and still foggy, and he was unable to get his bearings. *What is that faint light above me?*

He twisted against his restraints until he could see over his left shoulder. The sight of a gradually rising sun would normally give him comfort, but now he suddenly knew where he was. Execution Rocks! That wasn't the sunrise, but the automated beacon from the Execution Rocks Lighthouse.

Native American Indians would tie their enemies to these dangerous rocks during low tide and watch until they drowned when the waters rose.

During the Revolutionary War, the British learned this vulgar tactic from the Indians and chained war prisoners and Colonials to the rocks.

Here, hundreds of years later, Micko was facing the same horrific fate.

Think, man, think. When is the next high tide?

Micko knew he was doomed if the high tide came before sunrise. Here in the dark, boats were absent, but in the early morning, fishing boats would head out in this direction.

Stop.

Think.

Act.

The scuba diver's survival mantra came back to mind. He stopped fidgeting and calmed down. The worst thing he could do was to let a wave of fear panic him. If he did, then he was doomed.

He could tell his hands were bound by rope and probably his legs as well. It felt like something was attached to his hand bindings and connected to something in the rocks. He knew that fishermen hammered iron U-shaped anchors into the rocks so they could tie up their boats and fish near the fruitful rocks. This was illegal, but the fishing was phenomenal.

He guessed he was bound to one of these hooks, probably by plastic ties. If the plastic was the cheap household type, he might be able to wrench himself free by using all his strength to break the tie. If it was industrial strength, then he would die.

Micko pulled, pushed, and twisted with all his might to no avail. He didn't know how long he was in the water, and most of his strength was sapped. In addition, he was shivering and suffering from exposure.

Micko comically wondered, *which will kill me first: water exposure or drowning?*

* * *

Tall Man finished his nefarious deed and took a slow ride in the skiff. He was getting bored on the sailboat and decided to take some action on Hart Island.

Zodiac Man must have the treasure or know where it is, so Tall Man decided to enter the cave by the small cove. He rode slowly and quietly. He feared unseen rocks and being heard by island tenants nearby.

He arrived at his planned location without incident and beached the skiff. He didn't bother to hide it because he figured that if he won the upcoming battle, then there was no worry. If he lost, then who cared about the boat?

Tall Man crept closer to the cave opening and saw that a heavy steel door guarded the tunnel entrance. He thought for a moment and pulled out his flashlight. The beam caught the concrete wall that was dug into a rising cliff.

He looked around for any indication of an alarm system or trip wires or cameras. When he was convinced all was clear, he reached for the steel door.

He pulled slowly at first, being careful not to allow the rusty hinges to give away his presence. The door was heavy, but the noiseless hinges must have been oiled recently.

The door opened quietly but stubbornly, so he put some muscle into it and yanked the door open as wide as it could go. *Ping...ping...ping.*

"What the hell..." He shined his light on the concrete floor and watched as a hand-grenade retention lever bounced along the ground.

* * *

Micko saw a huge ball of flame erupt from the north end of Hart Island and a second later heard the blast.

He normally would be elated and hope that someone heard the explosion and would call the police and he might be saved. But Micko knew better. One mile to the west of Hart Island, Rodman's Neck sat on a small peninsula that jutted into Eastchester Bay.

Rodman's Neck is the location of the NYPD shooting range, aviation unit, and bomb squad. More than three hundred days a year, cops were shooting and qualifying with their weapons there. Thirty-five thousand cops had to shoot there each and every year.

The helicopters took off day and night, and the bomb squad detonated ordnance at unscheduled hours. Bombs and gunshots were common in this part of City Island and the surrounding areas.

The only thing this blast did was probably blow up his cherished kayak.

Micko twisted and looked over his shoulder again and saw that the sunrise was near. The water was rising near his neck. It was going to be a race: sunrise versus tide rise.

Chapter 16

"That was the north-wall booby trap!" Itchy cried.

Freddie grabbed an assault rifle, slung it over his shoulder, and stuck a Glock nine-millimeter pistol into his waistband. "Let's go."

Freddie led the way as the two traveled through twisting underground tunnels and archways. The route corkscrewed through the interior of Hart Island until they reached the end of the tunnel.

Itchy played his flashlight where the hand grenade had been propped against the wall. A huge hole was prominently displayed, as well as severe scorching to the walls leading to the exit door.

"Looks like most of the force was powered out the door," Freddie said.

They exited and saw the carnage. The lower half of a male torso was all that remained from the hapless victim. It was dark and wet outside, but blood spatter was evident.

"Itchy, fling those body parts into the deeper water. Eventually the outgoing tide and currents will wash them far away."

Freddie examined the steel door and said, "Thank God, the door was open all the way. The force of the blast shot right out the doorway and past the metal gate right into the chest of our intruder."

"The poor bastard never knew what hit him." Itchy laughed.

The two had a bit of difficulty closing the huge metal door, since the hinges sustained some damage. Eventually, Freddie was content that his lair was secure, and another booby trap was set.

The duo returned to Freddie's office, where they prepared for a quick getaway if it became necessary. In the darkness, neither of them noticed the gray kayak or Rosenberg skiff next to the Zodiac.

Freddie had a fortune in gold stacked in the orange Pelican case and scrap metal in the yellow one, just in case he had to use it as a ruse. Paranoia had a death grip on him.

He constantly checked the news. The takedown of his drug empire was a big story on most stations. So far, no mention of his possible whereabouts or his boat.

The fugitives weren't worried about the sound of the blast. Anyone who heard the noise would just assume it was more annoyance from Rodman's Neck.

Itchy began the subconscious scratching of his ears and the backs of his hands. Freddie said, "Go do your thing and relax. I've got everything covered here."

"Can I look at the treasure chest?" he begged.

"Do you know your way?"

"I'll do my best," he answered in a shaky voice.

Itchy needed a fix. He normally had a dose before he became unhinged, and that was coming close. He walked out of Freddie's office and into the unfamiliar labyrinth, looking forward to his peaceful escape from reality.

For the first time, he noticed the decrepit shapes of the hallways and rooms that lined the various corridors. He had trouble finding the room with the fuel cylinders and gold chest, and he accidentally entered a room that smelled like the one he was looking for.

This room was larger, and the smell was almost overpowering. He swung his flashlight to-and-fro and quickly realized this was not the correct room. Huge vats were lined up three deep along all four walls. Liquid was pooled at the base of many of the vats.

Too dangerous, he thought. *I'll blow this place sky-high if I freebase in here.*

His need to get high was now overwhelming, so he rushed into an adjoining room. This room had a distinct odor but not as strong as the other one. He looked around and saw numerous Civilian Patrol posters, helmets, air raid signs, and lanterns. The Cold War paraphernalia was incredible.

Itchy usually sat on the floor to shoot up, knowing he would fall over and pass out. This time, he decided to sit at a rustic metal desk with a rickety old chair. He intended to pass out and lie facedown on the desk.

He was shaking badly when he pulled out his packet of *King* heroin and his works. Unsteady, he lit a candle, cooked his dope, drew it into his needle, and found a working vein.

Itchy always wore long-sleeved shirts, so he didn't care about looking for veins in his feet or legs. In a few sweet moments, he entered the haven of euphoria. As expected, he fell face forward onto the desk, which dated back to one of the scariest moments in recent history: the Cuban missile crisis.

* * *

Micko was in a hellish situation but was lucky that the early morning calmed the waves. Earlier, the seawater was splashing against his chest and leaving a salty brine on his face. Now it just settled under his chin.

The Execution Rocks Lighthouse had become silent as the sunrise cleared the eastern horizon. Micko spun his head from right to left like a deranged pigeon as he attempted to view a passing ship he might contact.

Off to his right, he saw a magnificent sailboat pass between David and Columbia islands. The sailboat sounded an air horn, and a resident stepped out of the island house to speak with the boat captain. After their brief exchange, the boat kept sailing.

Water now crept up to his nose and sometimes splashed over his head. Breathing was getting difficult, and Micko had to time his inhalations lest he get a mouth full of water.

Suddenly, he saw a small orange coast-guard vessel speeding from the same location the sailboat came from. It was a new type of boat that was fast and looked like a speedboat on a Zodiac-like frame.

Micko could see the sunlight reflecting off the boat's chrome pieces, and it gave him an idea. He reached his head down to his neck and used his teeth to snatch the chain that held his silver Saint Michael the Archangel medal.

He twisted until he got the medal between his teeth and angled his head toward the rising sun. This became difficult as the water relentlessly rose and splashed down his throat. The sun was rising over his left shoulder, and the craft he was trying to signal was to his right. The sterling silver medal was reflecting, but in the wrong direction.

Micko was straining his neck, trying to signal, while brine washed down his parched throat.

Oh my God, is this how it's going to end?

He finally got into position where he caught a good reflection when he spotted a welcome sight. A blue-and-white police harbor unit boat was racing from the Queens County base in his direction.

Did somebody spot my difficult situation? Or was this boat meeting up with the coast guard skiff?

The racing police boat almost flew past him when the medal's flashing reflection caught the eye of the helmsman. He immediately downshifted and grabbed a pair of binoculars to take a look.

In moments, the boat inched up to the rocks that bound Micko, and a diver jumped in for the rescue.

Micko dropped the medal from his teeth and used all his energy to stand as upright as possible and try to breathe as water continuously splashed into his mouth.

"Well, what have we here?" Mike Crew joked.

"Get me...out...of here, you—" Micko couldn't finish as water engulfed his mouth and nose.

Using a pair of surgical shears, Crew had Micko loose in seconds.

"Now, what was that you were going to say? Something nasty, I bet," Crew joked again.

Crew dragged Micko to the boat's rear dive platform and watched as the waterlogged detective stumbled to climb aboard.

"My legs are freaking shot," Micko said.

"Probably just exposure. You'll be fine after a cup of Irish coffee." Crew smiled.

In moments, Micko was sipping coffee laced with Irish whiskey.

"What brought you guys out here?" Micko asked.

"The homeowner on Columbia Island complained about a cabin cruiser anchored too close to an underground cable running from David's Island to his generators. The coast guard took the call and boarded the cruiser and found two DOAs aboard. Then they called us. We were passing by when Gil spotted your signal. What was that shiny object, anyway?"

"My Saint Michael the Archangel religious medal."

"Well, he really is the patron saint of cops," Crew said.

While Micko enjoyed his hot and liquored-up coffee, Gil motored up to the *Who Nose*.

"Well, Mike Crew, good morning. Are you ready for this?" boomed Doc Dorrity, the skipper of the coast guard vessel.

"Good morning, Doc. So what do we have here?" Crew asked.

"Complaint was that this cruiser is anchored too close to land and an underground energy cable. We came out to investigate since unlawful anchorage falls into our jurisdiction. It appeared abandoned, so we went aboard, and our noses told us there was trouble on the *Who Nose*."

The coast guard skiff, *Rita II*, was tied up to the *Who Nose*, so Gil tied up the *Detective Luis Lopez* to the *Rita II*.

Micko dried off and borrowed a pair of NYPD Harbor Unit BDUs while his bathing suit and T-shirt dried in the warm sun.

Gil controlled the fifty-five-foot aluminum Gladding-Hearn with twin 740-horsepower Detroit Series 60 engines, while Micko and Crew transferred to the *Rita II*, a thirty-one-foot SAFE boat.

Well before they stepped aboard the abandoned cabin cruiser, they smelled the unforgettable odor of human decay.

Doc pointed toward the doorway leading to the galley and bunks. Although his legs were still wobbly, Micko led the way. The *Who Nose* was kept in immaculate condition, with the exception of the blood trail leading to the cabin. The deck was clean and freshly painted. The teakwood and brass accessories were polished, and the chrome fittings sparkled.

The cabin interior was as clean as the exterior. A small table with bunk seats was polished and neat. The head was clean, with a slight odor of Clorox. Almost all parts of this cabin cruiser were magnificent. The exception was the bunk room.

The smell of death was overwhelming, as were the flies and maggots. The two bunks were open, revealing the contorted corpses below. It was obvious that they had been shot multiple times, dragged, and dumped.

"Do you have any gloves?" Micko asked.

"Yeah." Crew reached into his BDU pants pocket and withdrew a pair.

Micko put them on, did a routine search of the bodies, and came up with their wallets and IDs.

"Oh my God," he said.

"What, what's up?" Crew asked.

"Remember the ferry incident, Mike? Well, both these guys were involved."

"These guys are corrections officers?" Crew asked.

"Yes, and although they were murdered, they might also be murderers," Micko said.

"Jeez, you can keep your job at homicide, and I'll stay here on the water where it's nice and safe." Crew laughed.

Doc climbed aboard. "Hey, guys. Gil ran the registration on the boat, and it's wanted. The all-points bulletin is for a drug dealer who is wanted for a series of murders. Apparently he knocks off his competition and is also suspected of selling hot doses of heroin to silence all witnesses. Quite a guy we're dealing with here."

Micko borrowed Crew's cell phone, called Chief Clifford, and updated him on the latest series of events.

"You gotta be fucking kidding me," he bellowed. "You now have about two dozen homicides on your hand, O'Shaughnessy, so stop lollygagging and solve this case."

Micko neglected to tell the chief about his overnight stay on Execution Rocks. No need to ruin his day any further.

He had to borrow Crew's cell phone because his phone, wallet, gun, and badge were in the well of the waterproof hatch of his kayak.

Micko returned to the harbor boat and changed back into his bathing suit and T-shirt. He asked Gil to drive him to his kayak on Hart Island.

On the way to Hart Island, Micko noticed a blue-and-white training sailboat anchored offshore. There was nothing unusual about this except for the number 217 on the sail. Training school and rental boats had sail numbers, not names. The number 217 bothered him, but he didn't know why.

Gil easily slid the police boat as close to the outer rocks of the small beach as possible. Micko spotted his kayak exactly where he had left it, climbed into the waist-high water, and thanked his rescuers.

It was now high tide, and the water went right to the edge of the tiny beach. Micko was glad he pulled his kayak far enough onto the beach. Otherwise, it would have been floating away on the tide.

He also noticed that the water neared a shadowy crevice at the base of an overhanging cliff. Naturally, he had to investigate. He went into the slight brush and saw a large metal door.

It was obvious that this door led to a tunnel of some sort that ran underground through the island. With the island's history of missile silos and underground launch capabilities, this would lead to unknown catacombs.

He was about to open the door when he noticed recent scorch marks around the concrete edges. *The explosion*, he thought. He was so overcome by his rescue that he had completely forgotten about it and failed to mention it to Crew or Clifford.

Micko didn't know what caused the explosion, so he decided on a safer course of action.

He decided to paddle around the east side of the island, beach the kayak at the sandy area, and continue his investigation topside on foot. He leaned into the kayak and removed his paddle, which he had pushed into the cockpit. He barely noticed that something else came out of the cockpit.

Micko reached down and picked up a severed hand. The wrist area was scorched, and the flesh was ripped, not cut. This body part was blown off. He was glad he didn't open the metal door like this poor soul must have.

Who booby-trapped this entrance? Are some homeless people living on the island or underground? Is the wanted felon who owns the Who Nose *hiding out here? Where did they get the explosives? Could they have been unintentionally left behind by the army?* Micko was confused.

He would have to do something about the severed hand, so he abandoned his topside search plans and headed back to his office.

He was glad that the hull hatch was intact and that his possessions were still in the waterproof bladder. Micko checked the cell phone and saw many messages, most from Esmeralda. His battery life was at 20 percent. He quickly contacted Mike Crew and asked him to call the registered owner of the training sailboat number 217 to find out if that boat was missing.

Somehow that sailboat, his kidnapping, and the severed hand were connected.

Why didn't my kidnapper just kill me and feed me to the sharks? Unless he was a romantic and wanted me to die in a historic place with a history of horrific drownings.

* * *

Micko paddled his kayak back to Gerhard's Marina and secured the small boat to the deck of the *Master Baiter*. He had plans that would require the use of both boats.

He walked to his kayak club next door at a brisk pace since he was still shivering from his long exposure in the water. After a steaming-hot shower and two more cups of coffee, the detective felt better.

Micko rode home to feed Mac and change into proper work clothes. He drove into work. He had numerous reports to write and phone calls to make, but first he would drop off the severed hand to the NYPD Crime Scene Unit.

"Well, what do we have here?" asked Sgt. Al Sherman.

"Hi, Al, can you print this guy and get me his pedigree information?"

With that, Micko produced the hand wrapped in a plain brown lunch bag.

"I gotta *hand* it to you, O'Shaughnessy. You pack a strange lunch," Sherman said.

"Sorry, but I can't stay and chat. I have tons of paperwork to do."

When Micko arrived at his desk in the 52 Squad room, he listened to the many voice mails on his phone.

Five came from the Corrections IG Tom Sullivan demanding DD5s and to be brought up to speed on the investigation.

Micko decided to make this his first callback. He would be pleasant as he blew off the IG with excuses about not having time to type, which wasn't entirely untrue.

"Hello, is this the IG's office?" he asked.

"Yes, this is Connie. How can I help you?"

"I'm Detective O'Shaughnessy, and I'm returning IG Sullivan's call."

"I'm sorry, but the IG is not in the office today," she said in an unsteady voice.

Micko picked up that something was wrong.

"Do you know where I can reach him? This is very important."

"Um, nobody knows where he is. He hasn't called, and he's not at home. His wife said he went out on an investigation yesterday and never returned."

Micko thanked her as he let this information sink in. Then it hit him like a bolt of lightning.

"Al, this is Micko. Can you run the prints off that hand into the Rikers Island guard's database? Also, any prints found on that *Who Nose* boat."

"Yeah, we have a nice blood print lifted from the latch on one of the bunk storage lockers where one of the corpses was stored."

"Great! Also, run that print through the Rikers database."

Micko's mind was racing at breakneck speed as he assembled his paperwork in order and began the laborious typing. Everything had to be in the absolute correct order, or a defense attorney could make him look like an idiot on the witness stand.

Several hours later, his phone rang. "Make it quick. I'm busy typing."

"Relax, Micko, it's Al. Your guesswork was pretty good. Both the hand and the blood print come back to a Thomas Sullivan assigned to the New York State Corrections Department. He's your murderer, and I assume your DOA."

Micko thanked Al and paced the room while the coffee was brewing.

"Man, you are wound up tighter than a spring," Gus said.

"This case is taking so many twists and turns. I hope all my perps wind up dead because I'll never get this paperwork in the proper chronological order."

Over coffee, Micko explained to his partner how he was hog-tied and left to drown at Execution Rocks and how he now knew it was the Corrections IG Tom Sullivan. Greed took an ugly toll on everyone involved in this case so far.

Tom Sullivan used his knowledge of the case to follow Andy and Manny and kill them. He probably also killed Lynch and made it appear to be a suicide. The crime-codes lab was running tests on saliva taken from cigarette butts in the lavatory where Lynch was found. Micko assumed that the killer hid in a bathroom stall waiting for his victim to drain the copious amounts of coffee he consumed. The killer tried to flush away the butts, but good CSI guys always find them.

"I'll call the lab and see if they were able to come up with any DNA from the cigarettes and if so, have them compared with Sullivan's DNA," Micko said to Gus.

"Well, partner, you just closed out three homicides. How many more to go, about a dozen?" Gus laughed.

"With some smart writing, I can probably do an exceptional clearance on the drowned prisoners. I just have to convince the chief of detectives that Andy Hastings intentionally killed them out of greed for the treasure."

"Good luck with that."

Micko spent the rest of the day typing up reports and fielding phone calls regarding the case. He finally had to update the chief on the events, including his arduous night tied to rocks in the middle of the Long Island Sound.

"You must be shitting me! That rat bastard Sullivan did this?" Chief Clifford was livid.

"Yes, he did. I just got a call from Mike Crew with the harbor patrol, and Sullivan used false credentials to rent a sailboat from a sailing school in

Manhattan. In my disoriented state, I remember seeing the number 217. That is the number on the sailboat's blue-and-white sail. Crew also found the stun gun he used on me and probably on Lynch. It's at the lab now for comparison."

The chief was pleased with the way the case was progressing. It looked like Micko would be able to close out all the homicides with some ingenious writing and a roundup of the Irish Patriot gang.

When Micko finished speaking with the chief, he ran over some loose ends of the case with his partner.

"Well, buddy boy, it's almost time for dinner. Where are you taking me tonight?" Gus asked.

"No time for you, my Rican pal. That long phone call I had was with Esmeralda, and she is cooking me a nice paella dinner at her place." Micko winked.

"What's the matter, she doesn't have an extra chair in her house?"

"Sure, she has plenty of chairs, but the dessert is just for me."

Micko placed the fresh DD5s into the squad lieutenant's in-box, where the lieutenant would sign them and forward copies to the proper agencies. Then he washed up and drove to his dinner date with Emmy.

* * *

Paddy Connolly was furious. He needed a boat so he could ride out to Hart Island and search for the treasure. He was depending on his pal Steve Wallace to take him and a few cohorts to do the job. Unfortunately, nobody told Wallace, and he was out on a bender.

Steve Wallace was the proprietor of the Sloop, a fine Irish tavern adjacent to the Hudson Park Marina in New Rochelle. Wallace owned a nice forty-foot Chris Craft pleasure boat.

Paddy intended to have Wallace drive the treasure hunters to Hart Island that afternoon, but the man was nowhere to be found. Wallace was known to go on a bender now and again, so the Irish Patriots sent a drinking party out to find him, and find him they did. Regrettably, Steve Wallace was unable to speak much less handle his boat.

Wallace was taken home, and Paddy warned his wife, Colleen, "He had better be fit by tomorrow morning."

* * *

Freddie knew his time in this hidden sanctuary on Hart Island was almost over. He was making phone calls and checking websites regarding his treasure.

"Itchy, we are packing up and moving right after our deal with the Dominicans. My cousin Burt will let us stay in his condo in Montauk. We will gas up the boat and ride there tonight. I have contacted two museums and three collectors who are interested in the pieces of eight and the doubloons. With today's heroin sale and cash, I can sit back and sell off a few artifacts a year for the next thirty years and still live comfortably."

Freddie had no intention of selling his final pure batch of heroin. He sensed that the Dominicans were planning to rip him off, so he decided to turn the tables on them. He was afraid to let Itchy know too soon. Otherwise, his junkie pal would need a fix, and Freddie needed his pal to be sharp today.

* * *

Micko dropped by a liquor store on the way to Esmeralda's house. He knew that paella was a mix of meat and seafood, so he was unsure if he should get white or red wine. He realized how little he really knew about his new flame. *I don't even know what kind of wine she prefers,* he laughed to himself. Being tactful, he purchased both red and white.

Esmeralda answered the doorbell almost immediately. She was wearing a bright, multicolored, off-the-shoulder blouse. She looked like a Tijuana peasant dressed for a fiesta, complete with flowers in her hair.

"Senorita, you look absolutely delicious. I hope the food is half as appetizing as you." He kissed her warmly on the mouth.

"Should I beware of Greeks bearing gifts?" she joked as she looked at the brown paper bag in his hands.

Micko joyfully pulled out the two bottles and asked, "Red or white, my dear?"

"Neither, *mi amigo*. I have a pitcher of homemade sangria," she said with a smile.

The two enjoyed a fabulous meal peppered with jokes and clever conversation.

"And now I have a surprise for my detective lover," Esmeralda said.

Emmy walked into the study and came back with an armful of ancient-looking schematics.

"You may have copies of the 1950s schematics, but I have copies that date to the Civil War."

Micko couldn't contain his excitement. "Where the devil did you get these?"

"I dug through the old manuscripts and found them this afternoon."

As Micko studied the schematics, Esmeralda looked over his shoulder, making soft contact with her face against his.

"Look over here." She pointed. "This is an escape route under the officers' quarters during the period when Hart Island was a training camp. The underground tunnel runs from the barracks to the sea right under this high bluff."

Micko studied the map and tried to mentally picture the area.

"This doesn't ring a bell," he said. "I've paddled around this island a thousand times and never saw an escape tunnel."

"That's because you were never looking for one, my dear."

Micko looked closer and realized that the escape hole would be farther up on shore than the watermark where he normally paddled. If there was a high bluff, the base of the hillside would be covered in vegetation, obscuring the opening.

"This is great! I'm sure this area would not be booby-trapped, and I could gain access to the catacombs beneath the entire island," he said.

"Booby-trapped? What are you talking about?"

Micko knew he had to confide in Emmy and told her about the harrowing night he spent tied to Execution Rocks and the explosion and the growing number of dead bodies.

She was aghast but quickly regained her composure.

"So, this is what you do for a living? You play cops and robbers with deadly results? I sure hope you get paid well."

Micko ignored her outburst and merely asked, "How do we know this escape tunnel is still there?"

Realizing the futility of questioning the common sense and logic of a cop, she answered, "Back in those days, the engineers ensured that things were made to last. The tunnel was probably built well. When the barracks were converted into other buildings over the course of the century, the foundation and tunnels remained."

"I know exactly where this is. This building is just south of the small beach that we use to gain boat access to the island. There is a huge abandoned powerhouse nearby, and they also had waste tunnels that ran down to the water's edge. I guess the escape tunnel ran close to the beach so friendly boats could rescue them."

Micko stood up from the table and drew Esmeralda close to his chest.

"Emmy, everything was wonderful," he whispered. "The meal and sangria were spectacular, you look like a Spanish angel, and the charts will make my job so much safer. What more could a guy ask for?"

Esmeralda whispered back, "I'm not done with you yet, buster. I read a lot more than old maps today. I found some dirty erotica and plan to experiment with my favorite detective."

The two adjourned to the bedroom where they explored new and exciting ways to pleasure each other.

* * *

Paddy Connolly was genuinely impressed when he received an early phone call from Steve Wallace. "Hey, Paddy Boy, I hear you been looking to hook up with me. Are you that thirsty?" He laughed.

Paddy smiled. He often got angry with Wallace but liked him above all his crew.

"I need your boat, boyo. Do you know the waters around Hart Island?" he asked.

"I do."

"Well, I need you to take me and a crew there in a few hours. Do you have that, you drunken fool?"

"Just meet me at the Sloop bar when you're ready, and I'll have the boat shipshape before you arrive."

Paddy hung up and called Donnie O'Neil. "Donnie Boy, gather the crew we talked about and meet me at the Sloop as soon as possible. Bring weapons, digging picks, and shovels."

* * *

Micko awoke early and shared a light breakfast and coffee with Emmy. They had a pleasant conversation about Esmeralda's emerging sexual imagination. They mutually agreed it was a good thing. They planned to meet for dinner that night unless some unforeseen circumstances occurred.

"Like what?" Esmeralda asked, displaying puppy-dog eyes.

Micko laughed at her attempt to pout. "If I make a collar on any of these murders, then I will be stuck at work and court for days."

"Who? Who are you going to arrest? All your murderers are already dead."

"Well, the Irish Patriots knocked off the Black Outlaws, and I still have to solve those murders."

"Are you close to arresting anyone, Inspector Clouseau?"

"Not right now."

"Good. Then I expect to see you tonight, right here, for another round of imagination and sexual exploration."

"Since you put it like that…" He let the sentence trail off with a laugh.

Micko bade his babe farewell, jumped into his car, and drove to the Gerhard Marina while listening to *Who put the bop in the bop shoo bop.*

He was glad Billy allowed him to use the boat after the rough night at sea, when numerous kitchen galley items fell to the floor. Obviously, Billy hadn't been on the boat to notice.

Micko replaced the fallen items and checked on his kayak. Convinced that it was secure, Micko opened the knapsack he had brought and dressed in old clothes for paddling and hiking through caves and catacombs.

The *Master Baiter* purred like a kitten as Micko drove it toward a spot marked on the ancient schematic Emmy had provided. The trip took less than fifteen minutes. Micko double-checked his location and dropped anchor.

He was about fifty yards offshore and one hundred yards south of the spot where boats normally beach at the small shoreline. The earlier boat creases in the sand had been washed away by incoming tides.

Micko gently eased his kayak over the stern of the *Master Baiter* and placed it outside the rear swim platform. He climbed onto the platform and smoothly slid into his small craft. Then he effortlessly paddled toward shore.

The detective found the cliff that supposedly hid the escape tunnel but was unable to see the exit point. Frustrated, he paddled into the rocky shore and carried his kayak on his shoulder until he found a flat piece of land.

He laid the kayak on the ground and removed the knapsack from the kayak's forward waterproof hatch. Soon he was walking through the thicket that caressed the foot of the sea cliff. He was surprised how far back off the shore this thick brush was.

He saw a discoloration in the wall of the precipice. He had to work hard to fight his way through the undergrowth to reach the cliff wall. There it was: a square hole covered with a rusty metal gate.

Micko was sweating and bitten by all sorts of mosquitoes and bugs, but he attacked the gate with vigor. Surprisingly, it became unhinged. The lock was firm, but the mortar that connected the gate to the wall gave way.

He stopped to remove fresh water and a high-density flashlight from his pack. After he quenched his thirst, he began to explore the inner linings of the passageway. But not before he checked his holstered .380 automatic pistol. It was small for carrying in kayaks and light clothing, and he hoped it had enough stopping power for whatever he came up against.

The tunnel was dank and moldy with an unpleasant odor. Cobwebs clung to his sweaty body as he crept deeper and deeper into the chasm. The walls were lined with metal pegs used to hold candles. With the dust and cobwebs, he was not afraid of booby traps. No one had walked through this tunnel in over one hundred years.

The floor was covered in an assortment of artifacts. Micko noticed old pencils, small medicine bottles, musket balls, the remains of a compass, and other oddities. He carefully tracked through until he was met with another eroded gate. It came apart like the first one.

This led to another much larger corridor that went left and right. Right was north, so he picked that turn and continued. He hoped that these underground corridors would lead him to the area of the Nike missile silos.

He didn't know how far he walked, but he eventually came upon a set of stone stairs that led upward. He stopped for a moment to think.

If I go up, I might come out under a collapsed building that might crumple down onto me. On the other hand, it might prove useful if safe.

Micko decided to take the chance. The stairs went straight up about twenty-five feet and led to a rust-covered platform with an empty doorway. Micko carefully looked around and entered the portal. He stepped into a huge room filled with the remains of oxidized machinery. The ancient machines were in such poor shape that Micko could not tell what this building once held. He did notice that it no longer had a roof or held the east wall.

He stepped past the antique trash and onto the topsoil of Hart Island. He was barely south of burial plot 440C. On his first trip here, he was riding in a van and didn't take much notice of the grounds. Now he noticed the huge white concrete slabs that covered the former missile silos.

Next to each silo was a metal-framed underground air turret. According to the schematics he read, these were access points for delivering fuel and missile parts.

The ones he saw were sealed well and didn't afford entry. It was obvious that he was the only one topside on the island, so he sat on the bluff he entered and looked out upon the sea as he thought about his next move.

* * *

Paddy arrived at the Sloop first and spoke with Steve Wallace's wife, Colleen, while waiting for the others. Wallace was busy washing up in the restroom.

Soon Jimbo Donaghey and Harry Kelly arrived, driven by Donnie O'Neil.

"Colleen, my lass, pour us some pints of Guinness like a good girl," Jimbo said.

"No! There will be no intoxicants until the job is done. Is that clear?" Paddy bellowed.

The Patriots looked at one another and at Paddy and nodded their heads in agreement.

"There might be a lot of manual labor involved, and there might be a dangerous aspect to this trespass. I want you lads to be strong and lively," he said.

Steve exited the bathroom and asked, "Are you ready to shove off?"

With that, the group walked the two blocks to the Hudson Park Marina and along the gangway to the berth of the *Unicorn*. Each Patriot was lost in his own thoughts. *Will we become rich or die trying?*

Chapter 17

Micko was somewhere between power thinking and daydreaming when he snapped out of his comatose state. A good-sized Chris Craft was approaching from the north end of Hart Island.

This was not unusual for a fishing boat of this type. This area was heavily fished, and pleasure boats often anchored there. The craft was approaching cautiously, but that was also common since the shoreline was rocky.

But something wasn't right. The cop's sixth sense kicked in. Micko dug into his backpack for his binoculars. When he trained them on the Chris Craft, he knew his intuition was right.

The digging tools were perched prominently on the stern seat cushions, and he saw at least one of the crew with a handgun in his waistband. *Men don't dig for fish or shoot them.*

Micko quickly looked around and took stock of the situation. *He was in no immediate danger. He had his ancient escape route to the kayak and anchored boat if he had to beat a hasty retreat. Why not just watch and see what happens? Maybe this crew will find the treasure, and he would follow or just call in reinforcements. That is if the phone works this close to High Tower Island.*

Micko watched as the Chris Craft ran up onto the sandy beach. All five men climbed out, but after a brief discussion, it appeared one would stay behind and guard the boat.

The others took shovels and pick in hand and began to spread out, looking in all directions. Some kicked through the sand while others searched slowly through the grassy knoll.

Micko realized that the shot-dead Irish did not relay the treasure location to these guys. They were looking about aimlessly until one member of the group called the others to his side.

One man was kneeling in the grass and showed an object to the others. Micko theorized that some spent cartridges were found and that the treasure hunters found the spot where their comrades were ambushed and killed.

This must be the Irish Patriots. *Wouldn't it be grand if they found the treasure and he arrested them and closed the entire case out*, he thought.

The Irish walked from the grass to the blacktop looking for signs of a recent burial.

Micko started to laugh to himself. *Go ahead, lads. Look for signs of recent digging. That must be the spot where the loot is buried. Hello! This is a graveyard, you stupid Irish bastards. There is evidence of digging everywhere.*

***

"Itchy! Itchy! Get over here," Freddie screamed.

Itchy was napping in the lounge while Freddie was doing paperwork in his office. "What's up, boss?" he asked while rubbing sleep from his eyes.

"Look, look." Freddie pointed to the security cameras.

Itchy immediately saw several men appear on each screen, and they were carrying digging tools and looking at the ground. It was perfectly obvious that these men had come searching for the treasure.

"What are we going to do?" Itchy asked.

"I was waiting for this, but it happened sooner than I'd like," Freddie said.

Freddie looked around the room and then said to Itchy, "Carry these bags down to the Zodiac. We will take them aboard the *Who Nose* and hide offshore until we meet the Dominicans."

"You mean the *On the Run*," Itchy corrected with a laugh.

They picked up the two Pelican cases and several duffel bags and walked through the underground corridors to the north point of the island.

When they arrived at the exit door, Freddie stopped. "Wait." He bent down and released the wire from the grenade lever. The pin had already been pulled, but the lever had to be removed to allow the interior bolt to trigger the spring that initiates the firing pin.

Freddie used the almost-invisible Spiderwire fishing line. He connected one end of the line to doors that could be moved open, and he looped the other end around the hand-grenade lever. When the fixed object moved, the wire pulled the lever loose, triggering the explosion. The weapon was harmless with the pin removed, unless the lever moved.

Freddie slipped the wire loop from the lever and opened the metal door. The two were loading up the Zodiac with the packages when Itchy cried out, "Boss, look! Your motorboat is gone."

* * *

Paddy was furious. Finding the shell casings stirred up his emotions. He liked J. K. and Waldo, and now they were dead. He was also frustrated, not knowing where the treasure was buried. *Is it hiding in a collapsing building? Is it in one of the thousands of grave sites? Is it in a freshly dug grave? How do I tell fresh from old graves?*

He looked around while trying to think. His men were watching him. They knew that looking for buried treasure in a graveyard was like looking for the proverbial needle in a haystack.

Paddy decided that this was an exercise in futility. He would have to coerce prison guards Andy and Manny to part with the treasure's location. He was reluctant to attack lawmen and bring negative attention to the Irish Patriots, but then he thought how much positive publicity and weapons he could buy with the treasure.

Is that gunfire? he wondered.

* * *

Freddie's heart sank. *What the fuck? How will I get out of here now? Think, think, you bastard, think!*

Itchy gazed at his longtime pal as Freddie rubbed his chin and stared off into space. Freddie slowly turned to Itchy and said, "Let's fight them."

Freddie quickly divulged his battle plan. Freddie would fire up the Zodiac while Itchy would sneak back into the catacombs and race to a special sewer shield that was located to the rear of the treasure hunters. Itchy was instructed to take one of the assault rifles with him.

With his phone in hand, Freddie would text Itchy when to open the sewer cover and spray bullets at the invaders. Presumably, this would scatter the trespassers. Itchy would then return to Freddie's location. Freddie was hoping the gunfire would distract anyone watching the interloper's boat. Freddie planned to kill anyone guarding the boat and then steal it.

"Hurry, Itchy. Run to the storeroom. Grab an AK-47 and a small pry bar and wait for my text."

Itchy ran as fast as he could. He stopped at the storeroom and grabbed the necessary items but made a quick detour before running to the sewer. Itchy ran to the room where the rest of the treasure was hidden in the chest. Freddie couldn't fit it all into the Pelican case, and without their own boat, they had to leave the rest behind.

Itchy quickly lit a candle, then rolled the chest out from behind the leaking fuel cylinders and filled his pockets as quickly as he could. *Thank God I'm wearing cargo pants and have plenty of pockets.*

Loaded down with gold and silver, he lumbered toward the sewer. He used the pry bar to ease the sewer cover loose. Freddie had used this spot to spy on the Rikers guards and their burial detail. Now Itchy was spying on the intruders.

* * *

Micko watched the confused Irish looking about erratically. Then he heard a motor and saw a gray Zodiac approaching from the north. The Zodiac swung near the small beach and slowed down. There was nothing unusual about this, except this was the same Zodiac that Micko had found before he was knocked unconscious.

A burst of gunfire erupted near the Irish. One man went down, and the others scattered into the underbrush and into crumbling buildings.

The Zodiac rushed up to the beach as the Chris Craft guard bolted toward the gunfire. When Wallace looked back at the sound of the oncoming Zodiac, he was cut down by automatic gunfire from Freddie's assault weapon.

Freddie had to act fast as he loaded his four packages on board the *Unicorn*. *Hurry back, Itchy, hurry back.*

Micko had seen the barrel flashes from the underground gunman's weapon and knew where he was. He instantly retraced his steps, ran back down the concrete stairway to the underground passages, and ran northbound toward the gunman's lair.

Itchy fired a full twenty-round clip at the intruders and fled, but left the sewer cover open as instructed. He also checked the various booby traps on his way to the tunnels that led to the beach area, intentionally dropping coins along the way.

Paddy jumped into a thick patch of brush at the first sound of gunfire. Donnie was struck in the legs and torso as he spun a dying jig before falling facedown on the dirt path.

The others sought cover in a run-down building.

"Paddy, are you all right, mate?" Jimbo called.

"Yes, but we lost dear old Donnie. Did you see where that sniper fired from?"

"I saw his muzzle flashes coming from the side of the road near that ditch."

"Everyone, converge on that ditch from all sides and take great care," Paddy ordered.

The remaining three reached the sewer without incident. Nobody took the time to check Donnie. They all saw his dance of death and knew he was a goner.

Jimbo arrived to the left of the opened sewer cover and threw a shovel at it. Silence. The shooter was gone. Jimbo carefully peered down the sewer shaft and spotted the iron rung ladder leading to the tunnel.

"That bollocks has a pair of balls taking on the four of us. He must be protecting the treasure down below. Everyone, down the shaft," Paddy ordered.

One by one, they climbed down the shaft and entered the catacombs. The Irish came prepared with brilliant flashlights and weapons. The digging tools were abandoned topside.

Paddy led the way into the smelly underground lair. There was complete silence except for the distant hum of a generator. Each of the Patriots had a deep feeling of helplessness and fear in this dark, claustrophobic tunnel.

The way was not clear to Paddy. The main corridor branched off into many directions of lesser paths. Paddy would reach a fork in the tunnel and play his flashlight in all directions to look for a lead.

His flashlight beamed on a shiny object. A coin. Paddy bent down to examine the coin when Harry yelled, "Here, here's another coin!"

The three Patriots followed the trail of coins like Hansel and Gretel.

"Don't bother to pick them up," Paddy said. "We want the mother lode."

Following the coin trail, the men quickened their pace until they reached a widening in the tunnel that housed many rooms with large metal doors.

"Beware, lads, that bloke may be leading us into another ambush," Paddy said.

He motioned with his hand to halt and take a breather. Each man drank from his water bottle while Paddy thought about their next course of action.

* * *

Micko ran carefully through the narrow passage until he heard the sounds of the Irish Patriots. He turned off his light and followed them from a distance. The darkness was eerie, and the smell was overwhelming.

Micko remembered reading about the rocket fuel used to prepare the Nike missiles for launch. Within the underground fueling area, the missiles received their liquid fuel and oxidizer—a potentially hazardous combination of jet petroleum, inhibited red fuming nitric acid, and unsymmetrical dimethylhydrazine.

This meant nothing to a Bronx detective except the words, "a potentially hazardous combination." *Is this what I'm smelling, or is it a combination of corpse decay and mold from a century-old graveyard?*

Micko began to perspire profusely, and he wondered if it was from the sauna-like atmosphere in the rancid tunnel or from fear.

The shaft widened where the Irish stopped to regroup. Micko observed the many rooms that lined this area of the tunnel and knew he was near the rocket launch site. These must be maintenance rooms, refueling depots, elevator equipment, generator rooms, and God knows what else.

Micko hid in an adjacent corridor as the Patriots deliberated. The smell emanating from a room near him was suffocating. The obnoxious odor almost knocked him over, so he decided to take a look inside.

The detective pushed open the heavy door carefully, remembering what had happened to Tom Sullivan at the north end of the island. The door gave way easily, and Micko froze at the sight before him.

Each wall in the room had stacks of cylinders lined up. The far wall had red canisters, the right wall green, and the left wall blue. The red canisters were all leaking fluid that spread to the base of the other cylinders. They in turn seeped small amounts of fluid.

Mother of God! The army left the hazardous rocket fuel components behind when they abandoned this launch site!

Micko was beside himself. He remembered reading that two large magazines had been built and that each could hold four Nike rocket launchers. They all had to have refueling stations and elevators to raise the missiles to a vertical launch position. *How much fuel did they leave behind? All of it?*

He was well aware of the army's propensity for withdrawing from sites, especially overseas, and leaving behind tons of valuable equipment. It wasn't cost-effective to clean up, pack up, and return it home.

But this is home!

Micko was disgusted at the thought that highly volatile fuel was sitting a mere quarter-mile offshore from NYC. Then it hit him.

He ran back the way he had come as fast as he could. The sniper was drawing the Irish into the tunnel while his cohort stole their boat. Now he knew why.

* * *

Itchy stumbled through the corridors under the extreme weight of the coins. He completed the tasks as outlined by Freddie. When he exited the scorched metal door at the north end of Hart Island, Freddie was there waiting.

He had the beautiful Chris Craft anchored ten yards offshore and had difficulty pulling his pal onboard.

"How did it go?" he asked Itchy.

"Great. They are in the tunnel now following the coin trail. It's just a matter of time before they set off one of your booby traps."

"Then let's get the hell out of here and meet the Dominicans." Freddie laughed.

* * *

Micko was coughing and out of breath when he came to a fork in the tunnel. *How can I not remember the way I came?* He took the left fork, and it unexpectedly brought him back to the abandoned building that he initially climbed up.

Sweating profusely, Micko exited the crumbled building and looked down from the cliff at his kayak and anchored boat. *Well, this is a fine mess. How do you propose to get down there? It has to be thirty feet below me.*

* * *

"Hurry, Itchy, pull up the goddamn anchor. We have to get out of here fast," Freddie said.

"I'm sorry, boss, but it's stuck in the rocks," Itchy cried.

Freddie knew Itchy couldn't jump overboard and free them, weighted down like he was.

"All right, I'll go into the water and unhook us," he said.

Freddie splashed around for a couple of minutes before the anchor gave way. Itchy hauled it on board and then hauled Freddie on board. In an instant, Freddie had the Chris Craft racing away from Hart Island for the last time.

* * *

The Irish proceeded with caution as they followed the coin trail, which led to a huge room. A pile of coins was lying at the jamb of the rustic door.

"Harry, no! Didn't your IRA training teach you anything?" Paddy scowled.

Jimbo opened the creaky door a bit as Paddy shined his light across the frame.

"Hello, thought I wouldn't see you, my little trip wire." Paddy gloated as he pulled out a Leatherman multitool armed with a wire cutter. One snip, and the wire fell free from the door.

Jimbo carefully opened the door and saw the hand grenade leaning precariously against the rear wall.

"Careful, lads, the pin is out, and she will be armed if the outer clip is moved," Jimbo said.

The trio looked into the massive room. A candle illuminated dozens of tall cylinders against the far wall and a desk and chair adjacent to them. They followed the coin trail and quickly located the treasure chest.

They rolled the dolly to the desk, and Harry and Jimbo attempted to lift the chest off the pushcart and onto the desk. The chest split and poured its contents all over the wagon. Harry and Jimbo immediately began filling their pockets.

"Stop doing that, you buffoons. Let's push the wagon back to the sewer we came down and then off-load it," Paddy ordered.

The men were giddy as they attempted to move the cart. One of the wheels was stuck. The three pushed and pulled until the wheel straightened out and rolled properly.

During the pushing and pulling, Harry bumped into the table, unknowingly knocking the candle to the floor.

"Let's get out of here and back to the sewer," Paddy said.

The trio made it twenty yards before the candle ignited the leaking fluid that covered the floor near the fuel tanks.

The fire quickly turned into a flashover, the near-simultaneous ignition of most of the directly exposed combustible material in an enclosed area. When certain organic materials are heated, they undergo thermal decomposition and release flammable gases. Flashover occurs when the burning gases give off a rapid buildup of heat.

In an instant, a searing wave of heat and flames engulfed the three Irish Patriots. The coins melted into a block of molten silver and gold.

Whoosh! The flames raced through the tunnels, seeking an air source and penetrating every inch of the underground complex. The force of the flames knocked over the hand grenade, and the last thing the Patriots heard over their anguished screams of pain was the first explosion.

* * *

Before they were one hundred yards away, the first explosion rocked the island. Then a series of small explosions followed by massive eruptions sent tons of debris sailing into the air.

Freddie and Itchy were first covered in dirt and mud. Then huge concrete blocks crashed into the water, barely missing them. They turned back to see flames escaping from every exit and entry point on the island. The firestorms licked one hundred feet into the air.

The explosions kept coming. Massive amounts of earth flew into the sky, carrying thousands of coffins and body parts with it.

Freddie had the *Unicorn* racing toward Sands Point, the meeting place with the Dominicans.

"Boss, I need a fix real bad, and I need it now," Itchy wailed just as skeleton pieces landed on top of him.

* * *

Micko was thinking about how he would get off this hellish island when he felt the first tremor. Almost instantly, he saw bright-blue flames shoot out of various openings in the earth around him.

They started at the northern part of the island and quickly raced toward him. Flames shot upward from a dozen underground turrets and delivery portals to the passages below the missile silos. A huge flame shot out from the sniper's sewer.

The entire island rocked as if it were about to take off for space. Micko stumbled and almost fell as a blast of fire crashed through the doorway of the building he was standing next to. He looked below the cliff and saw a huge wall of flame flare out of the tunnel that he used to enter the catacombs.

"Holy shit! I would have been incinerated if I was in that tunnel," he cried out loud.

The intensity of the blue flames shooting out of every island orifice increased as massive explosions crept toward him. The first explosions blew apart the concrete that was used to cover up the launch magazines.

Gigantic concrete blocks flew into the air and then came crashing down to earth, only to fragment across the road. Massive amounts of dirt were hurled in all directions.

Micko watched as each approaching explosion sent havoc in all directions. He knew that booby-trapped explosions must have ignited the dormant jet fuel. As the inferno raced from room to room, it ignited more combustibles.

The firestorm raged unabated underground and released its pent-up energy through sewers, turrets, doorways to the collapsed buildings and loading docks all over the island.

Micko was dodging concrete slabs, muddy dirt, coffins, and skeletons that dropped down like confetti. This was like a scene from Hades, and he had better get out before this furnace consumed him.

With that thought, Micko leaped off the edge of the cliff and tumbled awkwardly through brush and bramble until he landed on soft sand. Flames still shot out of the grating entrance that was the escape route for Union soldiers during the Civil War.

Bleeding from numerous cuts and scratches, he promptly grabbed his kayak, ran to the water's edge, and paddled away from this hellish island.

Micko had nightmarish debris falling around him as he raced to the *Master Baiter*. When he arrived, he merely threw his kayak onto the rear deck, pulled anchor, and motored away from the conflagration that was once Hart Island.

When he was out of distance from the flying debris field, he turned to look at the island, which was deteriorating like an erupting volcano. That once-historic island was now a hellhole.

When Micko turned from the firestorm and gazed forward, he saw the Chris Craft racing across the channel toward the Queens County mainland. The boat was far ahead, but Micko was determined to catch it. He opened the throttle all the way and made a quick call on his cell phone as the *Master Baiter* raced across the Long Island Sound.

Chapter 18

Freddie was having difficulty handling the large cruiser as he headed into a brisk wind that was kicking up a choppy surf. His long, blond, stringy hair waved about his face like a deranged flag blowing in the wind.

When the *Unicorn* passed the tip of Sands Point, they saw the Dominicans' boat, an unusual, dull, gray-painted Boston Whaler.

The usual routine was for Freddie to pull up to the Whaler nose first. He would then pull alongside the other boat as Itchy, in the rear of their craft, exchanged the heroin for the cash with the Dominicans in the front of their boat.

No one would take notice of the quick exchange, and Freddie would power away at a reasonable speed. The anchored Dominican boat would wait fifteen minutes before departing the scene.

As Freddie approached, he saw that the buyers were on edge.

I knew it. Those bastards are looking to rip me off. Well, I've got a surprise for them.

Itchy was unaware of his boss's intentions. He needed a fix, and he just wanted to complete this transaction and get away.

"*Hola, mis amigos, nuevo barco? Muy agradable.*"

"What did they say?" Itchy asked.

"They like our new ride," Freddie said.

Freddie handed Itchy the yellow Pelican case and motioned for him to hand it to the man with the black duffel bag. The transfer was made without incident.

Both groups usually inspected the contents of the bags they exchanged. If agreeable, Freddie would ride away.

This time, as the Dominicans opened the Pelican case, Freddie casually lobbed a hand grenade onto a rear seat cushion of the Boston Whaler, then he gunned open the throttle, causing Itchy to fall backward onto the deck of the *Unicorn* as it sped away.

The Dominicans were taken by surprise. They had intended to check the heroin and then open fire on an unsuspecting Freddie and Itchy.

The second the box was opened, and all eyes were on the contents. Freddie sped away. The Dominican gang saw that they were betrayed with a box of iron scrap and immediately grabbed their weapons from below the gunwale.

As they fired ineffectively at the fleeing Chris Craft, the pilot began raising the anchor to give chase. None of the drug dealers noticed the explosive device that Freddie nonchalantly dropped into their boat.

"What the fuck—" Before Itchy could finish his sentence, the summer day was shattered by yet another explosion.

Freddie headed his craft back around Sands Point, where they were out of sight from the exploded boat and potential witnesses. He knew that the four drug dealers would be killed immediately by the hand grenade and that the boat would burn, then explode and sink where she was anchored. He didn't need to observe this catastrophe. He needed to power to a New Rochelle Marina for gas for the long trip to Montauk.

Itchy was crying as he shielded his eyes from the sea spray that washed over the boat. "Why did you do that, boss?"

"Open the duffel bag. Go on, just open it," Freddie said.

Itchy opened the bag and saw that it was filled with a couple of old phone books and newspapers.

"How did you know they were going to rip you off?"

"I didn't become the heroin king without having good gut instincts."

Freddie felt invincible until he noticed a fast-moving boat trying to intercept him as he neared the New Rochelle Marina. He saw the conflagration that was once Hart Island in the background. *But who is this in the fast boat trying to cut me off?*

As the speeding craft came closer, it was obvious that the driver was coming for him. Freddie could see the man behind the wheel and noticed the determined look on his face. The man was wearing tattered clothing and was bleeding from many scratches and cuts.

This fool was on the island when it blew up, he thought. *If he's one of the Irish, he must be mad!*

* * *

Micko was so intent on catching up with the boat that he didn't notice his wounds. His mind was racing madly. *Who are these two guys? Are they the ones who booby-trapped the door that blew the inspector general's hand off? Have they been living on the island? Did they find the treasure? Was the treasure onboard that Chris Craft?*

The detective knew he had to catch them before he could question them. He was getting closer when he observed them interacting with a lackluster-looking Boston Whaler. The collaboration was brief as he watched the Chris Craft hustle away at a high rate of speed. Seconds later, the Whaler exploded in a crimson fireball, then the diesel fuel tanks burst into a wall of flame that instantly consumed the boat and burned it right down to the waterline.

Micko was furious. *I've had enough explosions for one day. This has to stop.*

He quickly closed the distance between the two boats. He could now see his opponents: a tall, ratty-looking thug was driving the craft while a shorter Peter Lorre type was nervously holding on for dear life.

The large Chris Craft did not handle well in the wind-driven waves, and the pilot was inexperienced with the craft and the unsettled water.

This gave him a distinct advantage with the speedier boat that he had managed to get used to. Micko made it appear that he was going to ram his adversary, but he turned away at the last second.

The Chris Craft pilot's eyes widened like a deer caught in the headlights as Micko flew harmlessly past. Peter Lorre looked like he was about to pass out.

The boat driver looked over his shoulder and barked unheard orders to his partner as he attempted to control his boat. The little man began to rummage through a large bag while trying to control his balance in the rocking boat.

Micko was trying to steer the larger ship toward the rocky area known as Chimney Sweeps. This is a stone arch with two large rock pinnacles that ancient mariners thought looked like dual chimneys. To Micko, they looked like goalposts on a football field of water.

The idea was to force the Chris Craft onto the rocks and disable it so he could effect an arrest of the two occupants.

Micko quickly abandoned that idea when he saw the small man lifting an assault rifle out of the duffel bag. Luckily, Peter Lorre kept falling onto the rolling deck of the recklessly driven boat.

Micko had one option, and it wasn't a good one. This case had been driving him nuts from the beginning. This day in particular had him acting crazy.

He slipped the lanyard connected to the boat's ignition key ring over his wrist as he raced toward the Chris Craft. When he was mere feet away, he turned the wheel hard left, until the two boats were side by side.

Peter Lorre was attempting to attach a twenty-round clip to the magazine holder of the weapon when Micko stepped onto the gunwale of the *Master Baiter*, jumped over the Chris Craft gunwale, and landed heavily on the *Unicorn's* deck.

Micko's balance was off; he had forgotten he still had his knapsack on his back. He fell heavily into the gunman, knocking them both down on the rocking deck.

"Shoot him! Shoot him, you fool," Freddie commanded over the cruel wind.

Micko got to his feet first and threw the weapon overboard before giving Peter Lorre a quick one-two punch that knocked him senseless. Tall rat man proved to be a more worthy adversary.

Freddie swung wild haymakers at Micko as Micko tried to pry him from the steering wheel. Micko dove at Freddie and grabbed him around the waist in an attempt to pull him from the steering console.

A mad wrestling match ensued as the boat picked up speed and the wind continued to whip the water into frenzied waves.

The *Unicorn* was headed straight for the east pinnacle of Chimney Sweeps as the wrestling match continued. Freddie watched in horror as they rapidly approached the towering rock outcropping. He made a final attempt to steer away from the inevitable crash when Micko grabbed him by his long hair and dragged him to the floor.

The two were rolling on the deck, kicking and throwing punches at each other when a wide-awake Itchy joined the fracas. The three maniacs fought furiously on the boat racing out of control until *bam*! The nose of the *Unicorn* struck the base of the east pinnacle, and the Chris Craft's stern swung up like a catapult, launching Micko and Itchy and all the boat's loose gear high into the air.

Micko crashed backward, high onto the stone monument, and bounced into the windblown sea. The backpack absorbed most of the impact.

Itchy was launched high into the air, missed the pinnacle altogether, and crashed into the ocean.

Freddie must have become caught under the pilot's chair and console because there was no sign of him being tossed from the boat.

The stern of the *Unicorn* crashed onto the crippling rocks clustered around the base of Chimney Sweeps and immediately burst into flames. The diesel fuel leaked out of the ruptured gas tanks, and orange flames licked the fuel spilling across the water-covered rocks.

Micko pushed away from the flames into deeper water and saw that the shorter man tried to do the same. There was still no sign of Freddie, so Micko assumed he was consumed by the flames.

"Help...gulp...me."

Micko turned to see the little man waving his arms helplessly and sinking. He tried to reach the man, but his backpack began to pull him under.

Itchy felt himself being dragged underwater. *The gold and silver!*

The treasure stuffed into his many pockets was weighing him down in the deeper water away from the pinnacle.

As Itchy sank deeper and deeper, he unbuckled his trousers and attempted to drop his pants so he could swim to the surface to fill his lungs with lifesaving air. Unfortunately, his pants could not fit past his boots. Itchy made a mad attempt to pull off his boots without taking the valuable time to untie them.

Itchy landed feet first onto the seabed as his lungs scorched from lack of oxygen. He looked down at the pants caught around his ankles and saw shiny pieces of silver and gold lying at his feet. His last earthy thought was, *I'm finally a rich man, and* this *is the way I'm going to be found.*

At first, Micko's knapsack was acting as a floatation device, but it became waterlogged and began to drag him down. He swam wide of the fiery East Pinnacle and climbed upon the jagged rocks of the West Pinnacle. He couldn't lose this pack; it held his gun, shield, and other valuables.

The saltwater stung the many cuts he had suffered leaping off the cliff from hell on Hart Island. Clinging to barnacle-encrusted rocks, he looked at the flames still shooting from the silos. *How long will that jet fuel burn?*

The explosions had ceased, but the inferno was impossible to look away from. There was no smoke, just blue flames licking the sky. He guessed the explosions were initially caused by the many booby traps.

The force of the explosions was greatly magnified by the jet-fuel fire and the lack of escape routes for the compression of the blasts. That was what blew the concrete covers off as well as other silo openings that were sealed by the army.

The thousands of graves and bodies had built up decomposition gases that made those sites especially volatile. Hart Island was a century-old time bomb waiting to explode. And explode it did.

Like watching a horrible car wreck, Micko couldn't look away from Hart Island. His mind raced as he tried to calculate how this could have been prevented. Could he have done anything to warrant a different result in this case?

His thoughts were consuming him when he heard a voice.

"Hey! There's no swimming allowed here. Do you want to get a summons?"

Micko turned around to see the *Detective Luis Lopez* NYPD harbor unit patrol boat ten feet away.

"Funny man, Crew, funny man," said Micko, glad he had the good sense to telephone Crew to help him intercept the Chris Craft.

"Do I have to come down there and untie you again? Is this some sort of S and M game you're playing, O'Shaughnessy?"

Gil brought the boat closer as Micko tossed his knapsack to Mike Crew. Then Crew helped the banged-up detective climb aboard.

"Did you run that burning boat aground?" Crew asked.

"Well, sort of."

"Where are the occupants, or should I ask?" Crew laughed.

"Is that also your handiwork?" He pointed to the blistering remains of Hart Island.

"Sort of, I guess," Micko said.

"And how many dead bodies has this case racked up?"

"Oh jeez, it must be near twenty by now…but it's finally over," Micko said.

"Whose boat is that?" Crew pointed to the *Master Baiter.*

"That's my ride. Do you like it?"

Micko explained to Crew that the boat had a suicide ignition switch. When the key is removed, the boat instantly stops. When he jumped from ship to ship with the lanyard attached to his wrist, the key came out, and the boat stopped. Micko proudly held up his wrist displaying the key ring.

"Very impressive, Micko," Crew said.

"Did you guys see an orange Pelican case?" Micko asked.

"No, why?"

"Oh nothing, I saw one fly out of the burning boat just as we crashed."

Micko grabbed his pack and searched through it until he found the water-proof pouch that contained his gun, shield, wallet, and cell phone. He immediately called Chief Clifford and gave him an update.

The chief listened intently without interruption. Most of what Micko was telling him accounted for the disaster occurring on Hart Island. When Micko was finished, the chief said, "What am I going to tell the mayor?"

"Tell him I'm taking a long fucking vacation! After I tie everything together with my DD5s, of course."

Chapter 19

Micko spent the weekend typing up DD5 reports and appearing at various hearings with the police commissioner, mayor, and army dignitaries. Everyone involved knew this was one huge clusterfuck, and they needed a scapegoat.

The police department considered him a hero while the US Army wanted to put the blame on him. During the army's inquisition, Micko asked just one question.

"General, what is jet petroleum, inhibited red fuming nitric acid, and unsymmetrical dimethylhydrazine?"

The hearing was quickly dismissed, and all charges against Micko were dropped. The mayor, police commissioner, and chief of detectives attended the hearing, giving Micko moral support during this witch hunt.

The mayor treated the foursome to an expensive lunch at Gallagher's Steakhouse in Manhattan. The upper crust ordered martinis while Micko ordered a Guinness.

"Now, tell me all about this case," the mayor politely said.

Micko took a long sip from his beer and looked each member of the party in the eye. He then told them the circumstances surrounding this bizarre case.

He explained how the convicts on burial detail accidentally dug up a pirate's treasure chest and that led to the drownings of five cons in their prison van.

He continued about how two prison guards sent opposing factions to recover the rehidden treasure chest and how the Black Outlaws killed two Irish Patriots after murdering a boatyard security guard so they could steal a speedboat.

Then he explained how the New York state inspector general, Tom Sullivan, murdered a coconspirator, Lynch Turner. Then the Irish took down eight Outlaws in their South Bronx Clubhouse after the Outlaws murdered two of the guards' wives.

Micko could see the mayor was having trouble keeping up with him. He revealed how the IG lay in wait on Hart Island to kill the two guards who found the treasure in the first place. He said avarice appeared to be the motive behind these twenty-one deaths.

The mayor almost choked on an olive when he heard the number.

Micko continued with the story: how he was kidnapped and left for dead by IG Tom Sullivan and how Sullivan was blown up by a booby trap set on Hart Island.

"Wait a minute," the mayor interrupted. "Booby traps! Who the hell is hiding booby traps?"

Micko relayed how a notorious drug dealer named Freddie and his cohort, Itchy, were hiding out on Hart Island producing mass quantities of high-grade heroin for offshore sales. The local police and detectives, along with the Drug Enforcement Administration, pursued them after an undercover agent helped bust up their local drug-distribution network. Freddie probably observed the guards hiding the treasure chest and took it into his underground fortress, which he booby-trapped.

The mayor's eyes were rolling either from confusion, the martini, or both.

"Continue, continue." He waved his hand.

Micko described how the IG hid the murdered guards' bodies on Freddie's boat so he would be blamed. He further told the mayor how the Irish gang of five descended on the island looking for the treasure and how Freddie's booby traps had engulfed the entire island in a cacophony of hell, killing the five and almost killing him.

The mayor gave Micko a fishy-eyed look as he downed his last sip and eagerly waved to the waiter for another drink. Micko smiled and drank more of his beer before continuing.

"Freddie and his partner in crime stole the Irish's boat, and I chased them as all hell broke loose on Hart Island. The jet fuel ignited, and I believe the rush of fire accidentally ignited all the booby traps as it sought air. It became a cascading rise of Armageddon as numerous canisters of jet fuel ignited and continued to burn throughout the day. While this was destroying the entire island, Freddie drove the stolen boat to a cove called Sands Point. Here, he threw an explosive device into the boat of some drug dealers, blowing them to kingdom come."

Chief Clifford said, "Mr. Mayor, we have since learned that four Dominican drug dealers were on that craft, and they were killed instantly. No loss to the world, since they were high-level dealers of street poison that kills our kids."

The mayor callously waved off the chief and motioned for Micko to continue.

Micko felt sorry for Chief Clifford and hastily ended his soliloquy by explaining how he chased down Freddie and the boat, making the boat crash and killing the drug dealers.

The rest of the meal revolved around the mayor's tactics to sue the government and the US Army for irresponsibly abandoning weapons of mass destruction along the Bronx coastline. The more he drank, the more he exaggerated the seriousness of the lawsuit.

Chief Clifford was having none of this nonsense and winked at Micko. "Sorry, Your Honor, but we must finish with this business in my office. The news media is all over it, and I must give them a logical explanation." He motioned to Micko to get up, and the two of them left, incessantly mocking the mayor on their way to the chief's office.

* * *

A week after the horrific events on Hart Island, Sister Immaculata was walking along a small beach in Oyster Bay. She was crying and wringing her hands in silent agony. She was the mother superior of her convent, which had branched out to become an orphanage. *What will I tell them? Where will the children go? Where will my nuns go?*

The Catholic Church was making cutbacks in nonproducing schools, churches, and other religious faculties. Her convent was on the chopping block, along with the orphanage. They had no way to raise money and relied solely on the generosity of a few private donors and the Catholic Church.

In angry frustration, she picked up a seashell and threw it into the calm surf. Then she noticed an orange object floating just offshore. The incoming tide was gently pushing it toward her. She waited patiently until the briefcase was near enough for her to grasp.

* * *

Micko was in his office catching new cases, as usual. All the hoopla was over. The 52 Squad was a busy place, and Gus was happy to have him back as a partner.

"Five two squad, Detective O'Shaughnessy, can I help you?"

"Hello, my name is Sister Immaculata. I read about you in the newspaper, Detective, and I hope you can help me."

"And I've read about you and the orphanage trouble, Sister. How can I help?"

"I know you were involved in the two boat explosions last week, and I just found a briefcase floating in the water. It has some valuables inside, and I'm wondering if it belongs to the people on either of those boats."

"Well, Sister, all those involved in the boat incidents are deceased. Why don't you bring the case into my office, and we will voucher it for one month? We will have to put out notices in the local papers that an orange Pelican case was found and that the rightful owner will have to come forward and describe the contents. If nobody does, then the case and contents belong to you, Sister, to do whatever you wish with the coins."

* * *

One month later, Micko met Sister Immaculata in the nuns' rectory chapel. They prayed together until Micko broke the silence. "Sister, it has all been arranged. The found property now belongs to you to do with as you see fit."

"Our rectory and orphanage will grow with the help of God and this gift." She said as she flashed a warm smile at the detective.

"Detective..." She hesitated. "I never described the case or contents to you...yet you knew."

Micko winked and rose from the pew.

With a knowing smile, Sister Immaculata said, "I'll pray for your safety and generosity, Detective."

"Cops can use all the prayers they can get Sister," Micko answered as he left the chapel.

About the Author

M ike Monahan continued the family legacy set down by his father and grandfather: he became a New York City police officer. Before retiring from the NYPD, Monahan earned the prestigious gold detective shield.

In addition to his career, Monahan's main passion is scuba diving. He has explored shipwrecks all over the world. From his waterfront condo in New York

City, Monahan combines his experience with police work and his passion for diving to create the adventures of NYPD detective Mick "Micko" O'Shaughnessy.

When Monahan isn't getting Micko out of his latest predicament, he's kayaking, fishing, cycling, golfing, scuba diving, or riding his vintage cruiser motorcycle through beautiful upstate New York.